# SAVAGE PAYBACK

## A Jack Calder Novel

## Seumas Gallacher

Published by Central Park South Publishing 2022
www.centralparksouthpublishing.com



Typesetting and e-book formatting services by Victor Marcos

ISBN:
978-1-956452-17-4 (pbk)
978-1-956452-18-1 (hbk)
978-1-956452-19-8 (ebk)

# CHAPTER 1

The walk from Green Park subway station took her five or six minutes each morning, depending on pedestrian traffic. This Tuesday was no different, except when she reached the junction with Piccadilly, the place was deserted. New Bond Street empty of vehicles was an unusual sight for Martha Compton. The normal daily clutter of cars and delivery vans had gone. Instead, yellow streamers taped off both sides of the street for a distance of a hundred metres. 'No parking' notices accompanied official roadwork signs from the local council to lay new underground pipes scheduled to start later in the day. Martha smiled.

*Wouldn't it be nice if they did this every day?*

At eight-thirty almost to the second, she stopped in front of the security-locked entrance to the branch of Moertens, keys in hand, knowing the timer on the door would release at the same time. Two of her staff waited for her, as well as the pin-striped security guard for the shop, the prestigious London branch of the Swiss-based jewellery chain. Around her, several of her peers, managers of similar high-value premier chains, attended to their own outlets. Official opening times varied among the dozen or so branches here, the centre for the high value retail gems and jewellery business in London.

For the first hour of the routine workday, staff retrieved merchandise from the inner vaults at the rear of the premises, made a double-person auditing on the tally stock sheets, and arranged the goods in the display counters, an art in and of itself. It wasn't normal to expect any clientele before mid-morning, after which New Bond Street busied with an assortment of potential customers, some with specific outlets in mind, others bustling from shop to shop, the 'jackdaw buyers' in trade parlance. None of these included purchasers from the low-spend range. A maximum of two or three clients were permitted entry at the same time in any one outlet. The security locks are controlled from inside the shops, released only to permit client buyers to enter and exit. The sun broke through the dark-tinged morning rain clouds, making the glare of reflected sunlight from the dampened street intrusive to the eye. Inside Moertens, Martha glanced up at the wall behind her to the oversized central display timepiece decked in diamonds and rubies ticking round to touch ten o'clock.

"We might be in for a fine day after all," she said to her assistant.

She never heard the response. A huge explosion erupted, ripping the front door from its hinges. The layered, reinforced entrance shattered into hundreds of pieces of malicious, glass shrapnel. The impact of the air compression from the blast stunned Martha's eardrums as she took in the horrifying vision of a man's bloodied arm enclosed in a pin-striped sleeve flying past her face. The security guard died instantly. She didn't know eleven neighbouring outlets were suffering the same fate. The shopping avenue transformed in seconds, resembling a blitzed war zone. A dozen simultaneous devices triggered at precisely ten o'clock had blown open the finest gems stores in London.

Moments after the blasts, four ambulances convoyed into the street, stopping twenty-five metres apart. From the rear of each vehicle, teams of men appeared, dressed in doctors' white lab coats and carrying leather medical-bags. They paired off to their target stores. Martha Compton, still reeling from the explosion, was further confused when the white-coated twins entered the shop. Her muddled mind didn't understand that the half-man, half-animal faces hid masked men. The intruders opened the bags and removed heavy mallets and pistols. The first man smashed the glass display top as Martha looked on in further astonishment. She reached forward to stop the attacker wielding the hammer, her courage answered with a blow to the face, smashing several bones and cracking her skull at the forehead. Unconscious, she crumpled in a heap to the carpet. The assailant stepped over her body to join his mate, continuing to smash the display counters, before clearing the jewellery pieces into their bags.

The looting repeated in every one of the shops, before the gang retraced their steps into the ambulances. They drove off while the sound of police sirens whaahh-whaahhed along Piccadilly, summoned by several internal alarms connected automatically to central security agencies. A slew of dead bodies littered the street where various front-door guard personnel had perished. Not all the stores were ablaze, but thick, black smoke billowed from some, the only sound the raucous concert of the fire alarms.

The SCO19, London Met's Special Crime and Ops teams arrived as reports of multiple bombings hit the newswires. The devastation meeting the first responders brought instant recall of recent terrorist atrocities in the capital. Not reminiscent was the report of four ambulances *already* at the scene as the attacks progressed and disappearing afterwards. The initial death count of eighteen rose over the ensuing week by a further five.

The value of the merchandise stolen from the twelve stores later tallied at over seven hundred million dollars, the largest single event loss in the industry's history.

# CHAPTER 2

In the offices of International Security Partners less than half a mile away in the West End, Jack Calder received the first message of something major developing in New Bond Street. Jack, an ex-SAS officer, and two former regiment colleagues, Jules Townsend and Malky McGuire, comprised the core team of the specialist security firm better known as ISP. Jules was the founder and chief executive of the company. Malky had been recruited at the same time as Jack when they'd demobbed together. They were all adept in undercover, black operations, but to the world the professional face of the company covered the efficient movement and safeguarding of high-value merchandise and personnel across the globe. Three of their client companies were among those attacked, including Moertens.

Jack summoned the other partners into the boardroom and relayed the information he'd just received.

"Sounds like a helluva commotion. Multiple hits on stores both side of the street. Bluudy mayhem," his Scots burr announced.

Nothing ever seemed to disrupt Jules Townsend's outwardly calm command manner.

"You and I will get down there now," he said. "Malky, you man the phones here. Call Paul Manning and tell him to join us. We need him to talk to his SCO19 pals to find out what he can from them. We cover Moertens as well as Cromleys and the Gemtec outlets. That's reason enough for us to stick our noses in. Try to contact their chief executives."

"On it," said Malky as his mates picked up their jackets and headed out. Jack held the door ajar, waiting for Jules to follow him.

Malky's large fist dwarfed the telephone as he tapped in the number for Paul Manning. Manning had recently joined ISP direct from his post as Head of Serious Crimes in the Metropolitan Police in London. The mobile line rang a couple of times before he picked up on the call.

"Paul here. What's up?"

"Hi, mate," the Irish brogue sang into his ear. "There's a stramash goin' down over in New Bond Street. Bombs, jewellery shops blown apart. The lads've just left. Jules says he'd like ye with them, tae tickle the ears of yer old chums in the SCO19 squad."

"I'm on my way. Catch you later."

The calls to the top men at Moertens and Cromleys connected immediately. Malky informed them ISP was already on site and they'd be kept in the loop for updates during the day. Each communication was short and to the point. ISP wanted to know how much value they estimated on site at the time of the robberies. And background details on all members of staff, although unlikely anyone in the stores would have been stupid enough to be involved and be hanging around when the explosives went off. Malky knew Jules Townsend's penchant for detail. Any absentees or delayed arrival of personnel? The police would check for the same things, but ISP needed to be at least as far up the curve.

Deryk Ostman, the chief executive and owner of Gemtec, the third name on the list, was based in Amsterdam. ISP had a strong relationship both personally and corporately with Ostman and his company, having successfully protected them against a major hijacking campaign several years earlier. Malky was unable to speak to Ostman. His assistant told him her boss was already on the way to the airport for a flight to London after hearing the news.

*Typical of him,* thought the Irishman.

Heavy cordons blocked off Piccadilly up to fifty metres left and right from the entrance to New Bond Street. Despite the security designation on ISP's Range Rover, access was denied. The orders were explicit, no vehicles other than medical responders and police authorised to enter the zone. Jules and Jack produced their identity cards and waited a couple of minutes before a uniformed sergeant waved them through on foot. The former SAS men had seen similar destruction many times before, but seldom in a First World setting. The devices which blew the doors shattered several front windows and debris was strewn across the pavements. Rescue ambulances lined up at the end of the street, with teams of paramedics fully engaged tending survivors, some with severe wounds, others suffering little more than shock and superficial cuts. Jack noted at least three bodies on the roadway covered with sheets, waiting for police clearance to move them to the morgue. Beyond any life-saving help, these corpses were now technically evidence. SCO19 and bomb squad members systematically moved from one outlet to the next, ensuring no surprise delayed detonations.

Jules pointed to the Moertens branch, the third store in from the junction. As they approached, stretcher-bearers exited the charred opening, tatters of an elegant marble and wood doorway. They stepped aside, allowing Martha Compton to be carried to the end of the street and a waiting ambulance. The paramedics walked alongside with medical drips attached to her arms. She was still unconscious.

"Morning, lads." Paul Manning entered the shop.

The former cop, well known to the police officers on site, hadn't needed to show his identity card. He peered at the remains of the entrance to Moertens. Having led SCO19 teams in the past, he was familiar with the after-effects of bomb blasts.

"Usual damage from a Semtex explosion," he said, pointing towards the streaks of black charring spearing outwards in radials from where the primer had attached to the bottom of the door. "Channelled like that, as easy as opening a tin of sardines."

"Yes," said Jules. "It's a professional job. I'll bet the other taps are exactly like this. We'll check them in a while. This took some helluva planning."

"These display tops are pretty thick glass," said Jack. "It would need heavy hammers to get through them." He waved towards the ceiling. "The CCTV cameras up on the corners look undamaged. The sooner we eyeball what's on them the better." He stepped back across where matted blood stained the deep, green carpeting.

"Hello, Paul," came a voice from the doorway. DCI Bob Granger from the Metropolitan Police stood framed against the outside glare. "These your clients? Hi, Jules, Jack."

He nodded to the others. Granger had worked a major case with ISP in the past, his respect for all three in the room mutually reciprocated.

"Yes, they are," said Jack. "So are Comptons and the Gemtec store. Okay if we keep looking? We'll not disturb your men."

"No problem. I think we're gonna need a lot of help. A terrorist hit like this'll get attention from the top. Wouldn't be surprised if the Government specialist undercover boys are on the way here even as we speak."

"They'd be wasting their time," said Jules. "This doesn't have the hallmarks of one of those. Tell me the last jewellery heist you heard of being a job for terrorists?"

"Hmm. Point taken. Anyway, I'm sure the spooks'll be crawling all over us with this. Well, you know the drill, guys. Don't touch or move anything. If you're asked to clear out, refer my name. You're good," said Granger, moving towards the exit.

"Thanks, mate," said Manning. "We'll catch up with you soon."

Martha Compton's surviving staff had been escorted earlier from the store. A beat policeman stood at the devastated entrance. Jules would have to wait to interview them after the official questioning. Along the street, similar officers were stationed on guard, some helping with the injured, others ensuring the forensic squads were unobstructed in their work. As Jack led the way to Comptons and then to the Gemtec store to survey the damage in each of these sites he took in the familiar, eerie silence blanketing the scene. He pictured the screaming and terrified shouting surrounding the place in the minutes after the explosions. That had given way to a subdued bustle as the paramedic and forensics teams went about their business. The usual crowd of reporters and television crews, corralled at either ends of the barricades in Piccadilly, found no direct access to New Bond Street. Above them hovered two press helicopters, one local and one international. The carnage would be screened on live feed constantly for the next few days.

The same radial markings on the entrance walls to Comptons and Gemtec showed the devices had been attached at the point of most vulnerability at the base of each door, just above the bottom hinges. Identical routines with the mallets in every store bore all the indications of first-class rehearsal.

Jules pursed his lips and nodded to Jack. "I think we're done here. Let's have a word with Bob before we leave."

Jack had worked with Jules for so long, he picked up on the look on his chief's face, coupled with the furrowed brow. Jules had caught something. As usual, he'd share whatever it was in his own time, probably back in the office.

DCI Granger was in conversation with a new arrival, the Assistant Commissioner of Police, Alan Rennie, distinguished by the silver braiding on his cap. Another friend of the security firm, the head cop had tracked the same early career as ISP's own Donnie Mullen, each of them highly respected law enforcement men cut from the traditional, tough, Scottish detective mould. Both had come from Dundee in Scotland to London. As the up-and-coming Head of Serious Crimes Division, known as the Flying Squad back then, Mullen had built a reputation as an uncompromising nemesis to the London criminal gangs, many of whom he had busted. A successful spell followed as chief of the Anti-Triad Unit in Hong Kong, before accepting early retirement to join Jules Townsend's outfit with responsibility for continental European operations. His close pal, Alan Rennie's rise through the ranks to his current position in the Met was equally stellar.

"Hello, Alan," Paul Manning addressed his former superior officer. "Bloody battleground this one, eh?"

"Too right. More than a dozen fatalities so far, and from what we can gather, a king's ransom in gear taken. You guys've checked out your own clients?" asked Rennie, shaking his head as another sheet-covered body passed by on a stretcher.

"Yes, we have," said Jules. "These are professional scores, Alan. I'd like to get copies of the CCTV film. ISP might be able to help your people."

"I'll try what I can with the tapes. Meantime, I've got to go talk with the undercover lads. That'll be a bundle of laughs. See you boys later."

Like all of them, the Assistant Commissioner had a difficult and busy day ahead.


Jules rang the private number for the new Stirling Lines at Credenhill in Hereford, the headquarters of the SAS. It was picked up on the first ring.

"Hello," said the polished voice.

"Hi, Mac. Jules here. How's your day?"

"Going well, Jules. To what do I owe the pleasure?"

Only a few people including Jules enjoyed access to Mac's direct line. Their close friendship dated back many years, to before Mac had lost his left arm in a grenade attack during a clean-up operation in Burma. Active intervention from Jules had persuaded the SAS to retain his fellow Major in the capacity of official record-keeper of all things relating to his beloved fighting division. His family name had long since eased into the background, but Mac's uncanny ability to surface facts and connections across the globe was legendary. Over several years, he'd developed his own cross-reference system on an old-fashioned computer, steadfastly refusing to be tempted into the latest new-fangled gadgetry. There was no better disciple of the 'if it works, don't fix it' school.

"I'm sure you've heard the news about the attacks in New Bond Street."

"Yes, I've seen the headlines. I thought you might be involved with some of the names, and half-expected your call. How can I help?"

"A couple of things to get us going would be good. Here's my initial thinking."

Over the next twenty minutes, the former officers chatted as Jules laid out his observations. Mac interrupted only twice with some thoughts of his own.

"Okay, leave it with me. I'll get back to you as soon as I've something relevant to tell you."

"Thanks. We'll be in touch."

# CHAPTER 3

Conversation in most of the offices in the financial district spun around the horrific atrocities a few miles away across the city. In the dealing rooms of stockbrokers and bankers, the share price fluctuations on the trading screens reflected the guesses and estimates of losses incurred and potential liabilities of many insurance companies, some accurate, but most, as usual, magnified by rumour.

The safest place to hide something is right under the noses of those looking for it.

The barred doors clicked behind the men, leaving them alone with the banker in the security area, three floors beneath the traffic in Lombard Street. The routine was simple. The officer had one set of operational keys to the boxes, the client had another. A third copy in a vault in the bank's remote premises twenty miles from London, served as back-up in case either of these sets were lost or stolen. The men each carried small suitcases of a reddish-brown, Moroccan leather, with numbered dial locks.

The bank man located the box registered on his control sheet, inserted the key, and tapped in the code. The taller client replicated the action with his own key and the separate number sequence. The empty security space swung open. The banker retrieved his key and retired from the room, leaving his customers in private.

As a matter of bank policy to provide absolute privacy to depositing clients, no CCTV cameras scanned this protected area. If there had been cameras, they would have captured the transfer of a series of cloth-covered packages from the small suitcases to the safe. These filled the deposit box almost to capacity. The door re-locked with the single sequence repeated by the client before buzzing the connecting line to release the inner gate. The whole procedure lasted no more than eight minutes. The officer noted the times in and out, and had the tall man initial the entries.

The transaction was the first in the banker's shift, as he covered the stretch from eight in the morning until he was relieved by an overnight watch colleague at six in the evening. Several other clients visited the vaults during the course of the morning and early afternoon, most of whom the banker recognised by face or by name. The clock ticked through lunchtime and two more customers appeared at the ante-room, tendering the number of another of the large boxes. This matched with his register and the procedure repeated anew. These were not the individuals who started his day for him. The deposit box also differed. While they proceeded with their business, something familiar occurred to the vault caretaker. He was sure the small, Moroccan leather suitcases were the identical ones carried by the morning visitors. Nothing illegal in that. Nevertheless, he made a mental note matching the numbers as the clients departed the vaults.

Two incidents like that may have been coincidence, but at five-thirty, a third pair of men arrived, with the key to a different space, with the same suitcases. After they left, the officer wrote down the sequence of numbers of the three depositary registrations. The six men appeared well-dressed and polite, with a distinctly foreign accent on each occasion, the origin of which eluded him. Perhaps he'd refer this later to his superior. He'd choose his time to do that. In the meantime, he checked the details of the deposit boxes again. They were opened in a trio of separate, corporate-holder names over a period of two weeks – less than a month before the deposits.

Clients have many reasons to maintain security boxes, perhaps some of which rested in the shadows of propriety but were of no direct concern to the bank unless formal, legal enquiries made it so. A perfectly valid explanation for the unusual sequence of visits the officer witnessed probably existed, but it niggled him.

*Well, it isn't my job to play the snooping sleuth. Best just stick to the standard policy. Customer confidentiality is paramount and all that. Nearly knocking-off time, out for a beer, then the subway home. They'll be showing a replay of the big match later.*

The shadow was still there, the seed planted firmly in his mind. He'd look out for these names again.

# CHAPTER 4

Deryk Ostman, third-generation owner of Gemtec, the second-largest gems and jewellery firm in Holland, had entrusted his group's world-wide security to ISP some years earlier. The faith in Jules and his team back then was reinforced with the successful undercover operation resolving a series of deadly robbery attacks on Gemtec by a Chinese triad organisation in the Netherlands and Hong Kong. The Dutchman was a strong, hands-on owner of the business and, as Jules had surmised and Malky's call had confirmed, the gem merchant's immediate reaction to the news was to fly to London immediately.

"Deryk's got Chuck Morrow with him for this meeting," said Jules, as he and Jack crossed the foyer of the Dorchester Hotel in Park Lane.

"Who's he?"

"He's the chief executive of Quantum Re-Insurance Group, one of the world's biggest. They've large-scale business interests in New York and here in London. Might be some opportunity for ISP if we play our cards right," he said, pressing the button for Ostman's floor. "He's also the chairman of the Society of Re-Insurance Groups, so I'm sure he's feeling a lot of weight on his shoulders today. His members'll be screaming at him for action."

Jack grunted. "Understood."

They stepped out of the elevator and turned left on the plush carpeting leading towards the Dutchman's suite. The expensive wall-hangings in the corridors reinforced the understated elegance of the hotel.

The 'Do Not Disturb' notice circled the doorknob, but Jules ignored it and pressed the doorbell. A faint chime echoed from inside. A few seconds later, the owner of Gemtec opened the door and greeted his visitors.

"Jack, Jules, hello. Come in please," he said, moving aside to let them enter a large sitting-room. The double-sized windows overlooking Hyde Park filled the place with light but kept out the traffic noise from the road below. A strong aroma of coffee indicated a percolator on the side cabinet near the leather-backed armchairs, with some used cups on the central table. A lanky figure turned from the window to face them. Dressed in a well-tailored business suit, a buttoned-down, collared, blue shirt offset with a badly matched tie, the semi-balding boss of Quantum Re-Insurance scowled across the room.

"You the security guys? It's been twenty-four hours since this shit went down. What've you people done so far? What've you got for me?" The aggression in the unmistakably American accent matched the rising volume.

Jules spoke before Deryk Ostman could intervene with any formal introductions.

"I presume you're Chuck Morrow. I'm Jules Townsend. I run International Security Partners. Let me be clear. We aren't contracted with you, nor your firm, so what we've got for *you* is precisely nothing. As far as what we're doing about this, as you ask, that's a matter between our clients, including Mister Ostman here, and some others involved in the mess yesterday." Jules raised his voice a little more. "In case you hadn't noticed, Mister Morrow, several people lost their lives in the attacks along with massive robbery on a scale hardly seen in this country or any other. The police authorities quite correctly are the primary respondents to these crimes. I consider it's of no *direct* concern to you what ISP's position is in all of this, but we're satisfied our protocols in each of our clients' premises matched the expectations and standards in our undertakings with them. These contracts don't envisage attacks of the type that hit them yesterday. I can understand as a re-insurer you and your fellow groups stand obliged to cover the losses incurred, and you're probably more concerned right now about covering personal and corporate asses than the people killed. Do I make myself clear?"

Jules held the American's eyes in a hard stare, before the executive shook his head and blustered, "You've no idea the kind of money we're talking about here. The last count is half a billion dollars and rising."

Deryk Ostman leaned forward signalling with his palms downwards for tempers to cool down. "Gentlemen, gentlemen. Please. Chuck, Jules is right. Nobody could've foreseen yesterday's events. Gemtec has worked with ISP for several years, and I can assure you these guys are the best in the business."

Jack glanced at his boss, noting his totally relaxed body language, and allowed himself a little inner smile. Jules Townsend backed down to nobody.

Morrow's eyes darted everywhere around the room. For a few moments nothing was said, then he sat down heavily on the chair nearest to the window. His shoulders slumped.

"I'm sorry. Completely sorry," he said. "I'm not usually such a prick. I haven't slept a wink since yesterday. My re-insurance partners have been on the phone non-stop the last twenty-four hours. Look, Quantum itself is into this for probably a coupla hundred million. It's a ton of money, but we've had these kinda hits before. We can ride with that. It's just…it's just…" his voice tailed away.

Ostman spoke for him. "Jules, the lady attacked in Moertens yesterday, Martha Compton, died of her injuries early this morning. She was Chuck's sister-in-law."

Jack blew out his cheeks softly.

*No wonder the guy was stressed.*

He looked over at Jules. His boss walked across to the American and gripped his shoulder.

"No apologies needed. We're sorry about Mrs. Compton, truly sorry."

"Would you like a Scotch?" Ostman asked Morrow.

"No thanks. I need a clear head today. Better with some more coffee."

"Allow me," said Jack, bringing the pot over. The atmosphere in the room had completely reversed. Chuck Morrow braced his shoulders, the chief executive persona reinstated.

"Deryk *has* told me about you guys, Mister Townsend."

"Jules."

"Jules. I think it might be useful for us to discuss with our members a paid role for ISP in this. The police'll do a good job, I'm sure, but from everything Deryk's shared, I think your skills and methods may be what's needed in this."

"A move like that would be sensible, gentlemen. From observations on site yesterday, I can tell you we're dealing with some clever operators. An extra layer of investigation might produce results a lot quicker. When will you let us know?"

"We're seeing the others after this meeting. We'll revert to you in a day or two if that's okay?"

"Fine, we'll talk to you then," said the ISP chief, rising to his feet and making for the door. "We've some other stuff to take care of. Thanks for the coffee."

* * *

"Slick as hell, sir. The planning must've taken months," said DCI Granger, placing the early report sheets across Alan Rennie's desk. "The council tapes they used to seal off the street were real. So far, all the witnesses can tell us is every attacker had a white lab coat and wore an animal mask. We've run the initial films from the external CCTVs from the night before the hits. They're too obscure to pinpoint faces, but they show a team of guys setting up the streamers and getting the explosive packets on to the doorways. Easy enough with adhesive. At this stage, from the four or five we've been able to zoom in on, it seems they even had the devices matched to the door frame colours. Almost impossible to spot unless you were specifically looking for them. We're scoping the internal CCTV stuff now and should be done by tonight."

The Assistant Commissioner nodded. "What about the ambulances?"

"They were from four different hospital services, all with large fleets. One ambulance from each went missing last week, not enough to raise any big alarms at the time. Who'd think of nicking ambulances, sir? Anyway, two turned up already, one in Hackney, and one in Kensington. No doubt the other pair will surface soon enough. The forensic lads are crawling all over the ones we've got."

"Fatalities?"

"We're up to twenty as of this morning. Something else to note, sir. These bastards fired at will. It strikes me they knew they were working to a tight timetable, and nothing was going to stop them."

"Among the villains we know, any ideas at this stage who this crew might've been?"

"None, sir. No local heavies are this good. A couple of the big lads from up north use shooters but not on this scale. Besides, they're not usually into knocking over jewel stores."

Rennie leaned back in his chair. "The Anti-Terrorist guys are picking their way through this lot, too. Let's see what they come up with."

"Ah, yes. On that score, sir, you remember Jules Townsend and Jack Calder turned up yesterday with Paul Manning? Jules told me he doesn't think this is anything to do with terrorism. Heists are not on the usual agenda for terrorists, he says. Can't say I disagree with him."

His chief smiled. "Not much gets past Jules Townsend. I suggest you might want to keep close to him and Donnie Mullen on an informal basis."

"Will do, sir."

As he left the Assistant Commissioner's office, Bob Granger surmised his boss would welcome the balance ISP could provide to offset the heavy-duty head-banging bound to come from the sessions with the official Anti-Terrorist spooks.

# CHAPTER 5

He flitted from one passport name to another as easily as changing his clothing. For twenty years a steady stream of assignments had fed his bank accounts well. He had more than enough to retire on in comparative luxury, but the money wasn't the reason he did this. From his first foray into the shadows, he'd relished the thrill of killing. The game. The chess moves. Creative ways of getting the job done. His aliases were known only to a handful of people and contacting him was difficult. Every step was made obscure, contracting his services a long process. He always delivered, this latest stroke his best ever. New Bond Street had lost a fortune. Now, two days after the attacks, the bank account showed a further twelve million added to the upfront fee of three million dollars. His paymaster on this job was well-pleased.

The strong caffeine hit compensated for the coffee's lack of taste. He finished the cup and neatly folded the newspaper before putting it back on the breakfast table. The three-star hotel in Kensington didn't match his tidiness. He always used a different place to stay in London, and never at the high-visibility hotels. The waiter brought the check, which he paid with cash, leaving a modest tip. Nothing too much, nothing too small, never anything to stick in somebody's mind after he'd gone. He rose from the table and made his way out of the restaurant to the front desk to settle his bill, also paid in cash. The limp in his left leg was hardly noticeable as he walked across a foyer carpet that had seen better days. The guest turnover in these hotels was high. One man with a slight limp wouldn't be front of mind for anyone.

He boarded the taxi with the small, black trolley-case holding what little luggage he'd brought on this trip.

"Where to, mate?" asked the driver.

"Heathrow."

"What terminal? Who you flying with today, Guv?"

"Terminal Four. Air Canada," he lied.

The journey to the airport took the usual forty minutes, filled by the cab driver chatting non-stop about the bombings in the West End.

"Bad business, Guv. Nobody's claimed credit yet. Unusual. The nutters are usually spoutin' all over the news claimin' dibs on it, but nuthin' so far. On the telly last night, the cops don't seem to be sayin' nuthin' either. Really bad business, eh?"

He grunted in reply at intervals in the driver's diatribe. They drew up opposite the entrance to Terminal Four and he handed over a few notes.

"Thanks, Guv. Enjoyed the chat, have a good flight."

The driver waved. The taxi disappeared and he made his way into the building. A left turn took him to the elevators leading to the floor level for the connection to Terminal Three. A few minutes later he presented his ticket for the British Airways flight to Gibraltar, homeward bound. The other pieces of the plan he'd outlined to the paymaster were about to be set into play.

*  *  *

The two shift partners made the handover to the relief-duty men just before midnight and ambled along the alleyway to the food stalls. The *dai pai dongs*, the licensed street vendors, were crammed with customers, even at this hour. The owner of the pitch beckoned as the pair approached, pointing to the prawn fritters and cha sui pork strips. In double-quick time, a couple of plates appeared on the table to the side of the stall, backed up with small tripod chairs. Two bowls of steamed rice and glasses of dark, jasmine tea completed the order. The street crackled with noise from the other stalls lining both sides of the roadway, a mixture of loud, Cantonese voices and a hodgepodge blend of local music channels blaring from the vendors' radios.

A motorbike roared into the street. The rider and his armed, pillion passenger wore hoods. The burst from the Uzi submachine gun ripped into the two patrons and the stall owner, splaying their bodies across the wooden counter, scattering the uncooked meats and fish pieces to the ground. No-one else was targeted. The reaction from the startled bystanders and nearby customers was rapid and instinctive. They disappeared as quickly as possible. Nobody wanted to be around if these guys came back, or when the police arrived.

The market had lost a seller. The other two victims would no longer be serving ISP Hong Kong's office as security guards. A posse of street cats cleaned up the food bounty littering the pavement. Very little goes to waste in Hong Kong.

* * *

She cleared the paperwork into the filing drawers and locked them for the night, the month-end accounts for ISP's Berlin office completed. These past few evenings had meant a bit of overtime work to get them done but had paid off. Tomorrow, she'd print them out and start the next month's client invoices. Her husband wouldn't mind her being a little late getting the dinner ready when she got home, as he understood how much she enjoyed her job as head of accounting.

Most of the employees in the building had left an hour or two earlier and the second-level basement car park was almost empty. Her small Volkswagen tucked in near the corner, close to a green Ford van parked in one of the general visitor spaces. She pointed the key remote at her car and clicked the locks open. As she was getting in, the side door of the van slid back, and she caught the slightest movement of an arm with a gun pointing her way. The silencer reduced the sound to a couple of whiffs as the bullets entered her head and neck. The transit drove off, leaving her body slumped halfway into the front seat of the Volkswagen.

* * *

The Calders had moved to the sitting room after dinner when the phone rang. Being nearer, May-Ling picked up.

"Hello, this is May-Ling Calder."

A torrent of frantic Cantonese met her ear from the Hong Kong operations manager. May-Ling was his natural first point of contact at Head Office as she had general responsibility for the Asian offices. Despite Jack's scant knowledge of the language, he understood the repeated word for 'dead', and his ears pricked up. His wife spoke quietly into the receiver. She managed to calm the caller enough for him to understand her immediate response to put the Hong Kong office and all personnel on red alert. Her face looked grim as the call ended.

"Two of our guards have been shot dead at a *dai pai dong* stall in Kowloon," she said. "I've ordered a complete lockdown. We'd better ring Jules."

Jack's reply was cut short as the phone shrilled again, and this time he picked it up.

"Jack Calder."

Donnie Mullen's east coast accent came on, the stress in the Scotsman's voice evident, unusual for the former street-hardened cop.

"I've just had a call from Germany. Our head accountant's been gunned down in the office car park. I lunched with her the day before yesterday. The woman wouldn't hurt a fly. She was talking about how difficult it was to balance being a mother and an executive. Jeez. I'd better get over there as soon as I can. I've ordered all personnel to stay home until further notice."

Jack felt a shiver. He understood operational killings. Those had cause, but having their own support people attacked violated a whole different code of conduct.

"Shit. May-Ling got word a couple of minutes ago. Two of our people've been killed in a drive-by shooting in Hong Kong. What the hell's going on? I'll talk to Jules right away, but yes, I think you should get to Berlin tonight. We'll head over to the office now. I guess we'll be there overnight with this. Let us know what's going on as soon as you can. I'll put out an all-offices signal red as well. Tread careful, big man."

"You too. I'll be in touch."

May-Ling never felt out of her depth in the company of the three former commandos. She'd spent an intensive part of her own career for several years combating heavy-duty criminals in the Anti Triad Unit in Hong Kong. Here in the London boardroom, she sensed again the invisible switch thrown when these men faced the ugly side of their business. Her husband, a fair-haired, blue-eyed, six-feet two, Glasgow tough man, with a gentle nature she loved and few apart from herself ever saw, sat across from his life-long, fighting buddy, Malky McGuire. The Irishman stood four inches smaller, with a stocky, muscular frame toned by regular exercise. Jules Townsend, the ex-Major who'd employed each of them, entered the room and took his seat at the head of the table. At six feet tall, Jules always appeared relaxed, belying his tenacious fighting abilities, a leader with a well-earned reputation as a ruthless field commander. His leadership qualities included a legendary, almost obsessive regard for detail.

*Detail saved lives. Detail took the lives of opponents.*

Jules leaned forward and asked, "Have you informed our other offices, Jack?"

"We've spoken to all of them, yes. High alert everywhere."

"I don't expect any more hits right now," said Jules. "We would've had them by this time, but the red alert stays until further notice."

Jack watched the jaw tighten and the slight twitch at Jules' neck, the sign he and Malky had come to recognise over the years. The suppressed anger of a man who tookany attack on his people anywhere in the organisation as a personal issue.

"Who's talking to the families?"

"I touched base in Hong Kong," said May-Ling, and Donnie'll be seeing the family in Berlin in a while."

"Any ideas where this is comin' from, Jules?" said Malky. "Who've we pissed off this time? These are obviously related attacks, right?"

"There's no doubt they're related and I've a strong hunch who's involved, but I'll get back to you on that after I check out one or two things. Meantime, we've got Chuck Morrow due in shortly. Jack, you can meet him with me."

# CHAPTER 6

The bags under Morrow's eyes betrayed his loss of sleep. A sober, black necktie replaced the one from the previous encounter, indicating family mourning.

"Make yourself comfortable." Jules indicated a seat and pushed some coffee towards their visitor. "Anything fresh from the police?"

"It's a bit too early to expect significant news. A guy called Granger's being very helpful," said the American. "He's keeping me abreast of things every few hours."

"Bob Granger's a good man. Trust him. How did your insurance partners respond the other day?" asked Jules, switching to the real reason for Morrow's presence.

"As expected, there's a lot of confusion among the member groups, including whether or not the cover is terrorist related. Most large clients nowadays require a clause covering that, so it's a moot point. The merchandise valuations vary, but the aggregate tops seven hundred million bucks and maybe up to another thirty million." Morrow paused and topped up his coffee cup.

Jack held out his own for Morrow to refill. "How many groups are we talking about?"

"Nine core re-insurers, and as I told you the other day, my company, Quantum, covers the biggest exposure, two hundred and fifteen million. The smallest is in for twenty million. Quite a range."

"What did you decide?" asked Jules.

"The discussion didn't take long. Deryk Ostman relayed his experience with you guys and of course your company name is familiar to most of the players in the business. We've agreed and I've been instructed to offer you a contract by the Society as a whole, the members will be liable pro rata for your fees and expenses."

Jules nodded. "What kind of scope and success measurements do you have in mind?"

Morrow coughed. "That's the tricky part. Getting all these guys in one room to agree on anything is pretty much like trying to herd cats. What we kinda hoped you might accept is a double-layered deal."

Jack put down his cup. "Go on," he said. "You want all the stuff back, gift-wrapped, right?"

Morrow spread his hands and smiled. "That's a perfect-world scenario, Jack, and we're practical people. We'll be lucky to sniff any of this in the short term. We don't think this stuff'll be offered into the market as the made-up articles. Only a minimal mark-up in the pieces covers the craftsmanship costs in jewellery. The gems can be removed and sold separately. The intrinsic value varies with the universal trade prices for the individual stones. The gold, silver and platinum settings are tradable too. A huge black market is always available for these and for the gems themselves. Of course, we'll factor in an element of pay-out based on percentage of goods recovered, if any."

"What's the other consideration?"

"A proposed success fee for nailing the people responsible for this. The Society would generally provide a certain sum, paid out to whoever's instrumental in bringing the perpetrators to justice."

"Isn't that what the law's there to do?" said Jack.

"The law's the law, Jack. I repeat, my members have been in this game a long time. Most of us acknowledge the need occasionally to move in ways other than the usual legal routes."

Now the discussion had taken a different turn.

Jules intervened. "Let me understand clearly what you're saying. Your people would be pleased to have the jewellery returned, but may have a keener interest to ensure the guys who did this could *never* do anything like this again? Am I correct?"

"Ten million dollars says that's right, Jules."

Chuck Morrow wasn't smiling any more. He reached out for his coffee and sipped, watching for Jules' reaction, before adding, "If you accept the engagement, I'm authorised to handle all communications with you. The contract would be worded in a way that broke no laws, but we want justice. *Proper* justice."

His words hung in the air, the meaning unambiguous. Jack nodded to his boss.

"You've talked us into a deal," said Jules, standing with an outstretched hand to the insurance chief. "Get something to me as soon as you can to document this."

"Thanks, I'm pleased and grateful. Good day, gentlemen."

# CHAPTER 7

Less than an hour after the jet touched down on the short, saddle runway in Gibraltar, he was sitting with his private banker in the secluded salon reserved for High Net Worth clients of Reliance Bank. The connecting flight to Casablanca didn't depart for another few hours, leaving ample time to discuss the investment portfolio profile for the recent addition to his funds. The general manager knew him as Robert Cavendish, but guessed his client answered to other names. All paper correspondence from the bank awaited collection, with any urgent communications transmitted in code to a forwarding email link. The non-distinctive, casual clothing dressed the body of a man who kept himself at a high level of fitness. The bank officer couldn't recall ever seeing the tight line at his lips graced by a smile. The plain, tanned face bore no beard nor moustache, no scars nor distinguishing facial features, except for his eyes. The piercing, dark grey eyes.

*Like those in the sort of painting that followed you around a room, never directly looking at you, but always watching you,* the officer thought.

There was the noticeable, but slight limp on his left side when he walked into the office. He delivered instructions quietly, which strangely imparted a mild sense of menace. Whatever his client's background, the executive treated him with the utmost courtesy. This man's investments now accounted for more than forty million dollars of the funds under management at Reliance. The discussion lasted less than an hour before the client left the bank and hailed a taxi for the airport.

# CHAPTER 8

It took months for Ahmed Fadi and Manuel Estrada to come face to face. Intermediaries from both sides postured and wrangled about how to meet, where to meet, who should attend with them, and when. In the end, the top guys decided themselves. Just the two of them. Neutral ground. For their first meeting they'd agreed on here, the presidential suite of the Four Seasons Hotel in Boston. For Fadi, talking cost nothing. His hold on the drug trade and prostitution rings was solid across two continents, in Asia and Europe. Estrada matched him for power in North and South America.

The suite was booked in the name of one of Estrada's front corporations, as were the empty suites on either side. The rooms were swept for surveillance bugs, a matter of routine. All three had double guards in the hallways with concealed weapons. Their masters were careful men.

Fadi and Estrada could mutually afford the other the courtesies attendant with positions of enormous power and influence. The first hour was absorbed by the customary, polite exchanges as the two became more relaxed in each other's company. They weren't direct competitors in any arena, which made conversation easier.

Fadi leaned back in his armchair and addressed the issue head on.

"I won't deal in America, my friend. Too many places for things to go wrong. My channels are in Europe and Asia, so I'm not sure how you'd think we can work together."

"It's *because* your network's outside of the States I wanted this meeting. I agree with you," said Estrada. "It's tighter than ever over here.

People everywhere screwing up the business. I can't figure if it's the DEA becoming smarter or the street guys getting dumber. Maybe a combination of both. Whatever, I think this is a good time to explore other options. I'm looking for fresh outlets and you're the best where you operate. With my strong supply lines, I feel we'd work a great partnership."

"I'm flattered but must say my organisation is pretty settled. I don't need to spread myself any further than I am now."

"I'm aware of that. However, let's talk straight. We're both businessmen. It's no secret you took a big hit when the cops whacked your boat in England last year. That kind of thing gets to all of us. Shit, my business is constantly getting knocked off by the DEA. Spillage is part of the cost of being in this game, and yours was huge. Tying up together is a bit like a mutual insurance policy. We help each other out, make sure supplies keep regular. You know what I'm talking about."

The Mexican had touched a nerve, but Fadi responded with a faint smile. Less than a year had passed since an operation led by Jules Townsend and the ISP squad just off the English south coast had resulted in the loss of half a billion dollars of street-value heroin, plus the impounding of his prized, luxury super-yacht, *The Constellation*. The blow hadn't been fatal to his business, but it *was* a major setback.

"As you say, we all have our little incidents to cope with. Your own recent path hasn't been smooth either," said Fadi, alluding to a couple of large DEA interventions at the border in Texas with the publicised seizures of costly shipments of cocaine. "We're not here to score points on each other, my friend. Tell me what's on your mind."

Estrada opened the small folder by his side and took out a few sheets of blank paper.

"I'm a simple man, Ahmed. I don't like things too complicated. Here's an approach to consider," he said, writing several headings on the notepaper. For an allegedly uneducated man, Estrada's command of facts and figures was impressive. Like Fadi, running an empire such as his took a focused mind, with ruthlessness an imbedded trait.

"Your supplies are from Afghanistan, Myanmar, Nepal and Pakistan," he went on. "Mine are from Colombia, Peru, and Mexico itself. Your transits channels are Turkey, Eastern Europe and then Western Europe. We use many points along the USA border, Canada, Panama, and Hawaii. You're mainly heroin. Me, cocaine, heroin and meta." He paused and looked at Fadi.

"How am I doing so far?"

"You should've been a college professor," said Fadi, smiling. "But with all these things, the devil's in the details. I could see how operational matters would be covered. The big question is how to share the profit? Many a marriage ends in divorce, almost as it starts, over money."

"We create a separate business we own and run as partners."

Estrada leaned forward with his pen again and sketched out a rough diagram.

"Our existing operations feed into the new one, so all the supplies and costs are identifiable. The money chain we both track together. Equal shares, a case where one plus one'll make much more than two."

Fadi steepled his fingers to his lips.

"I like the idea of spreading the risk, but it's never quite as easy as you've got on paper," said Fadi.

"That's why we ease our way forward, test the waters, so to say. What's to lose?"

"Seems reasonable. When do you want to start? And how?"

"A shipment of cocaine's ready to send to Europe now. Do we let our people do a trial run together?"

"Hmm." Fadi nodded to his proposed new partner. "I presume your senior men are here with you, as mine are. Why don't we bring them into the discussion, find out how they'll coordinate? No two outfits ever function exactly the same."

"They'll operate as we tell them. With us driving them, we'll make it work."

"Agreed. Let's get their heads together for the next day or two."

He stood and offered his hand to the Mexican.

"Now, time for some lunch, don't you think?"

Ahmed Fadi had several aliases, with legitimate passports for all of them. Well over fifty years earlier, his name at birth in the Slavic town of Sarajevo had been Viktor Bodan. The records showed Bodan headed a command of guerrillas in the fiercest fighting of the Balkans conflict of the eighties. Rules of conventional warfare were ignored as a savage culling of enemy population horrified the rest of the world. Entire villages of men, women, and children were wiped out as the ethnic purges took their toll. Bodan led much of the action. The story was that the urban commando perished with several of his unit in the midst of street fighting in Tuzla. But his body was never recovered for identification and burial. The reason was simple. During the confusion in the conflict, the guerrilla leader just walked away. Possessed of guile and the loyalty of the remnants of his fighters, Bodan reinvented himself, changing his name to Ahmed Fadi. Over time he built a criminal operation that feasted on the turmoil in the region. The same ruthlessness he carried over from the ethnic warfare helped him establish a stranglehold on the drug supplies from Afghanistan. A strong trade in prostitution rings and human trafficking created more cash for the main business, the movement of heroin into the European markets beyond the near East.

In Europe, Fadi steered clear of the Italian *mafiosi*, ensuring no overlap of territorial coverage. Inviting unneeded complications with powerful rivals was not his style. The control Estrada brought from the Americas made it worth the time to learn what his Mexican counterpart had to say.

# CHAPTER 9

"It's slow, sir. The lab tests confirm Semtex-loaded devices. There's no way in hell to trace where they came from."

DCI Bob Granger placed the folders on his side of Alan Rennie's desk.

"The bomb squad people say they were professionally rigged, and it didn't need too much on the doorways to blow them."

"What about the casualties?" said his boss. "Did the survivors give us anything to go after?"

"Nothing sensible. The teams hitting the stores did their homework. Each pair had one guy to take care of resistance while the other smashed the display cases to grab the jewellery. Smooth as hell, sir. The noise from the blasts deafened the staff. No-one recalls voices. Here's some photos of the damage."

Granger spread a few coloured glossies on the desktop. The Assistant Commissioner walked round to join him, peering at the montage of devastation. The sickening images of mangled shop interiors and bodies pictured some of those killed while others bore the bullet wounds from close-range pistol shots.

"What else've we got?"

"Only three of the CCTV cameras give us clear images. The explosions blew the rest off-screen. Nothing shows except the animal masks, white coats, and doctors' bags."

"Is Interpol linked in if the stuff turns up abroad?"

"Yes, sir. The usual wires. We've made progress on descriptions of the major pieces, lots of them, but the trade guys think the stones'll be broken out and peddled that way. Nothing's surfaced yet."

"Okay, good work. I've got the Anti-Terrorism chief, William Lang, due in a few minutes. Stay with me for that."

As he finished speaking, the intercom buzzed on his desk.

"Yes?" he said, pressing the interconnection button.

"Mister Lang for your ten o'clock appointment," the voice announced.

"Thanks. Send him in."

Some people have the ability to rub others the wrong way, the capacity to unsettle, to appear aggressive without the vocal edge often accompanying the trait. Alan Rennie had met with Lang on three or four previous occasions, after incidents involving the threat of terrorism in London. Each time resulted in the same feelings in the Assistant Commissioner, an instinctive sense of distrust, a nervy, creepy feeling at the back of his neck. The language was always civil, almost too polite. Rennie was an old-school police officer; a straight talker, a 'get to the point directly' sort of cop. Lang had risen very quickly through the streamed channels in the bomb squad and special incidents units, due largely to political string-pulling. The early gossip mill tied Lang's career to a half-uncle in the upper levels of government, a persistent, if unproved, rumour. The fact remained that the dapper William Lang shared little in common with the current Assistant Commissioner.

"William, good morning," Rennie greeted his visitor, knowing he'd never be addressed as Bill or Willie. William it was. "This is Detective Chief Inspector Bob Granger. I think you two've met before?"

"Yes, the other day in New Bond Street. Good morning, gentlemen."

Rennie gestured towards the sitting area away from his desk. Lang placed himself in the middle seat, brushing imaginary crumbs from his trouser leg.

"I have to confess I'm getting considerable pressure from our lords and masters at the Home Office to get some early wins on this," said Lang smoothly, sounding like the least pressured person imaginable. "The Minister is taking a direct personal interest. As you can understand, the press and the Government Opposition party are playing merry hell."

The Home Office was the arm of the Government responsible for internal security and Anti-Terrorism. Lang reported directly to the Minister.

"He's wondering why it's taking so long for any significant leads to surface. Of course, I tried to tell him these things aren't as easy as he thinks, but with a dozen shops blown open and the deaths and injuries splashed all over the newspapers, the public outcry is getting louder by the hour. He's growing quite uncomfortable."

Alan Rennie struggled to appear calm but seethed inside.

"I'm glad you relayed to the Minister how complex this is. We've already established the use of Semtex explosives and we're checking every piece of CCTV film still usable. A long process, I'm afraid. Your instant wins for the Minister may not be possible. Would you like to share with me what, if anything, your Anti-Terrorist team has achieved so far?"

Bob Granger suppressed a smile at the emphasis his boss placed on the words, 'if anything'.

*Alan Rennie wasn't about to let this slime ball mess with him.*

"We're combing the usual lists at the points of entry, airports, cross-channel ferries," said Lang, not taking Rennie's bait. "Plus, the suspected cells and possible feeders in-country. You don't need to concern yourself with my patch, Alan. I'm only trying to protect you from unnecessary nastiness from those feeding information to the Minister."

*Like hell you are,* thought the Assistant Commissioner.

"Much appreciated," he said with a half-smile, standing up and offering a handshake. "Let's keep in touch on progress."

The meeting over, Granger was pleased.

*His boss still held control, showing the upstart it was time to leave, time for Alan Rennie to get on with his own programme.*

# CHAPTER 10

Mac accepted the long-standing invitation to come to London for dinner with ISP. This provided quality time for him to give the team feedback following the telephone chat with Jules. Not all the squad were able to be there. May-Ling had flown to Hong Kong to attend the funerals of the murdered Chinese guards while Donnie Mullen undertook a similar mission in Germany.

The former officers were always pleased to have Mac around, but the mood was sombre as they sat down to eat in their private salon in the Army & Navy Club in Pall Mall, not too distant from the terrible events of the previous week. Jack and Malky flanked their ex-colleague-in-arms, sitting opposite Jules and Paul Manning. Mac placed his squared file-box attaché case on the right-hand side of his chair, next to his good arm. The perfectly ordered notes and files came from a precision born not of cleverness, but of necessity, as any other process proved impossible for him to work with. A one-man division, he had a genius of memory coupled with an innate sense of how facts and events connected. His findings would be invaluable to ISP.

The history of achievement and heroism in naval and military engagements stretching back for centuries spilled from the portraits stacked along the club's corridors. Many of the staff came from families with service backgrounds. The forces look after their own. From several previous visits Jack recognised the two waiters serving their salon and exchanged friendly nods with them. Even within the club's rankings, special respect attached to the SAS.

The usual, excellent dinner fare preceded the main agenda of the evening, the briefing from Mac. The waiters topped up the coffee and liqueurs and left the room, closing the door behind them. Mac snapped the attaché-case lock open and withdrew several sheets of paper and a couple of photographs.

"Gentlemen, as you know, I asked Mac to have a dig through his treasure troves to help narrow down a few things he and I discussed the other day," said Jules. "From the look of his luggage, I believe he's brought his usual magic to bear. Am I right, Mac?"

"I'll let you be the judge when we're done, but, yes, some success, I think," he said. "First of all, the optimal positioning of the Semtex packages on the doors is general manual stuff for any professional saboteur. You guys got that in your own training courses. However, there aren't too many organisations with a similar sort of grounding, and most of them would be black-operational military units. Maybe the Israelis, the American Seals and one or two others in Europe, but limited, yes."

The nods around the table showed complete agreement, including from Paul Manning, who'd dealt with incidents involving explosives during his time with the Bomb Squad in London.

"Determining the intermediary source of the Semtex is almost impossible with so much available on the black market if you know where to go," said Mac.

He looked around at his dinner companions and found no disagreement.

"One distinguishing element stands out, however, in what happened last week. I understand the packages colour-coordinated with the doorways they were planted on. That little detail is the most important clue of all."

Jules met a murmur of recognition from Jack and Malky with a knowing smile.

"Rikko Duval," the Scot and the Irishman said at the same time.

"Go to the top of the class, gentlemen," said Mac. "Rikko Duval, indeed. Born Frederick Pierre Duval to a French mother and English father. Came through similar training to yours. SAS field officer, tough as nails. A genius with explosives. The colour camouflage is his own specialty. His fingerprints may not be on this lot, but his stamp certainly is."

"He's in the SAS?" said Paul, his face showing surprise.

"Used to be in the SAS," corrected Jules, no longer smiling. "He went rogue many years ago. There was a nasty double-murder involving a girlfriend and another man. Duval reacted badly to being thrown over for the new guy. The pair were blown to pieces starting the guy's car outside a cinema in Barnet. The signs pointed to Duval, but he disappeared before any arrest could be made. The authorities never found him."

"I remember now," said Manning. "Before my stint in the Bomb Squad. Some of the senior guys still talked about it a few years later."

Malky turned to Mac. "D'ye think he's still around then? Why would he be involved in this caper?"

"Not around in England perhaps, but alive, yes, despite unconfirmed reports of his death a long time back," said Mac.

"Rumours said he hired out as a high-priced mercenary. Is that right?" Jack asked.

"My records have several incidents involving a guy who'd more or less fit Duval's description. All highly specialised situations, and most of them with explosives, although not always exclusively so. If it was Duval, the story went sour for him in Lesotho. A hit on a school bus carrying a couple of dozen kids on a day trip. Most of them died in the blast, those who survived suffered dreadful injuries from a simultaneous double-detonation, front and back of the bus, maximum impact. The target was the daughter of a local politician, the contract financed by an opposition candidate."

"How did it go sour?"

"The cops didn't take long to patch together the thread and arrested the bomber at the airport. The name Duval wasn't mentioned, but it's unlikely to have been anybody else. We made enquiries from our end, but the silence from Lesotho was deafening. The local boys wanted to deal with things their own way. A couple of months later, the guy vanished into thin air and whatever they'd done to him in prison left him with a badly damaged leg."

"These photographs, Mac. Duval, I presume?" said Jules, pointing to the glossies.

"Yes. A much younger version of course. Here." Mac handed them across the table. "He overlapped with you in the regiment, didn't he? Two years, as my files tell me."

The librarian extraordinaire never made mistakes.

"Yes," said Jules. "He and I seldom saw eye to eye. No outright disobedience in the chain of command, but always an undercurrent with him. He served under me for almost two years, then transferred to the explosives specialist team. Sharp as a pin mentally, constantly on edge, maybe a hidden chip on the shoulder."

The piercing dark-grey eyes of a young man gazed directly into the camera from a face with no distinguishing features. Jules handed the photographs across to the others.

"We've no idea where he might be now," said Mac. "If he's working under contract, it'd be a better tack to try to nail down who's hired him."

"Jeez. That could be anybody, couldn't it?" said Malky.

"Not just anybody," said Jules, "It'd be somebody who's either very greedy, or pressed for a huge amount of money."

"Well, put me at the top of yer names," said Malky, laughing. The others joined in the laughter, including Jules.

"If we cut you out of it, Malky, it leaves a short list of possibilites," said Jules. "Who's lost a ton of money recently?"

Jack answered the question for the rest of them. "My God. Bluudy obvious, isn't it? The lad who's shipment we scorched last year. Right, Jules?"

"He'd be top of my guesses. He lost half a billion dollars street value in heroin in one hit, enough to make anybody in a hurry to get that back somehow, don't you think? The drugs business thrives on cash. Cash is money, or goods easily convertible to money. That's what we've got here."

Jules leaned back in his chair.

Malky blew out his cheeks in pretence exasperation.

"Why am I the only idjit in the room wi' no brains? How do ye think like that, Jules?"

"A working theory for now," he said. "Another bit of the jigsaw makes me believe Duval's involved."

"Let me guess," said Paul, putting his coffee cup back on its saucer. "The attacks on our own people are linked with this, right?"

"The thinking of a policeman," said Jules, nodding his head. "Cause and reason, followed by effect. Yes, I think it could be tied in, and probably is."

"Bejeezus, will yeez slow down. Ye've lost me," complained Malky, looking from Paul to Jules.

"You might be right," said Jack, picking up on the train of thought. "But I don't think they were payback killings. They'd have come after *us* if that was the case. They could've been meant as distractions, red herrings."

"Precisely," said Jules. "Intended to ensure ISP was otherwise preoccupied while the main game goes on unhindered."

"Do you think the drugs lad would be so clever?" Paul joined in again.

"No. But Rikko Duval is *that* smart. If it *is* him, he'd know we'd be involved. He's an intelligent thinker, a bit of a twisted genius. The invisible hand playing chess with other people's lives. My guess is he's also got payback on his mind, but not the same as the drug chief. He's still pissed at the SAS. He might be having a go at us and getting paid handsomely for doing something else at the same time."

"How do we fight this, then?" Jack asked.

"We do what Mac advised. Find the man with the money and trace backwards, maybe not such a needle in a haystack. Alan Rennie's sure to have the Met plugged in to the Interpol guys. Something's bound to surface on the jewellery. This mob needs cash, fast. My bet is the gems'll be in the market sooner than you think."

The dinner conversation lapsed into lighter issues. Malky continued to shake his head, admiring the thought processes Jules Townsend never failed to display.

*If this Rikko character wanted a deadly game of chess, he'd more than meet his match in my man, Jules.*

# CHAPTER 11

The first whispers surfaced ten days after the heists. Feelers for takers of stones in Russia, Turkey and Switzerland sent small ripples into the gems markets. The trade was aware of the sheer volume of the merchandise stolen from New Bond Street and, as in every walk of life, the industry people liked to gossip. When a few identified polished diamonds turned up in Istanbul, the merchant who'd bought them pleaded innocence with the Interpol agents. The threat of prosecution produced a name of a well-known intermediary in the black market. The intermediation in all kinds of stolen goods in this vibrant crossroads between the East and the West made up a significant part of the economy. Most of the activity was too small to have the authorities waste resources and time on the individual players. Medium and large-size illegal business was supported by *bakshish*, regular bribe money payments to multi-levels of police. The same pay-off system blanketed the constant flow of illicit drugs, mainly from Afghanistan. The intermediary dealt on behalf of several principals, the main one being Ahmed Fadi. The undisputed drug king was a recognised name, but not a familiar face to the authorities, as he always worked exclusively through middlemen.

The underworld's Turkish police protection made enforcement difficult for the Interpol team. A raid on the intermediary's home without alerting their local counterparts yielded the agents more of the stones. While grilling the broker, the lead Interpol man mentioned Ahmed Fadi as a possible principal, prompting a startled reaction. An instant look of fear accompanied by too vehement a denial of even knowing his name indicated the strongest pointer to Fadi's involvement, although not sufficient to take it further at that stage in the case. In the meantime, the intermediary was not arrested, the strategy being to let the man back into the mainstream and tracking him undercover to find out where he'd lead them.

The information fed to Alan Rennie in London, then relayed directly to Jules Townsend.

"Thanks, Alan. Appreciate your keeping us posted. How're the investigations going?" Jules asked.

At the other end of the secured line, the Assistant Commissioner sounded under pressure. "Slow, I'm afraid. Apart from this heads-up from Istanbul, nothing's showing anywhere else yet. Are you familiar with this guy, Ahmed Fadi?"

"The name means nothing to me, but I think he may know us."

"Oh?"

"He might've been the top lad whose shipment we nabbed last year. We're gonna have to do some digging on him."

"Well, that'd certainly open up a whole new dimension to this. I'll have the Interpol people in Turkey ask around a bit more. Right now, I've got the bug of all bugs chasing my ass. Lang from the Anti-Terrorist outfit, plus the Government banging at me for results. Anything you can find for me would be a big help."

"Understood. I'll get back to you soon. Goodbye," said Jules, putting the phone down.

# CHAPTER 12

The early morning hours, lying awake with the dawn not yet near, always nagged the worst. The painkillers gave relief for a while before the gnawing ache took over. The reconstructed knee functioned perfectly well except for the limp, but the restorative work on the ligaments and nerves, operated on too long after being smashed up in the prison yard, made a fully painless recovery impossible. The spasms bit deeper, and he relived over and over again the attack which had left him unable to walk for weeks. Understanding the mental post trauma syndrome came easily, handling it not so simple. At first, the absence of rational thinking scared him, until he realised it was an exaggerated fear response. These initial recall sequences reinforced a flood of paranoia until eventually he determined to overcome them by reprogramming the memories. The irrational reaction gradually subsided, replaced with a resolve to exact a bloody payback for the betrayal and abuse he suffered at the hands and boots of the guards in the prison. This morning, as with most others, he began the flashback of events, knowing this therapy gave him the sense of regaining control over something that had terrified him at the time.

*These people were serious. Money, big money, paid in advance, non-returnable. A politician's daughter. Easy target. School bus. No security to worry about. Installing the devices, a piece of cake. The timers did their job. Now get on the plane and back to Casablanca. Then the world went pear-shaped. The airport locked down in minutes as several trucks of armed soldiers swarmed the place. They knew who they were looking for. Faced with a dozen guns, he realised he'd been set up. Bastards. Despite not resisting, they beat him up severely on the way to Lesotho's infamous maximum-security prison in Maseru. There was no trial. Daily, he expected a bullet in the head which never came. No lawyer to represent him. His name just another alias on a false French passport. The first couple of weeks he languished in solitary confinement, not even given time out to walk around the yard from where he could hear the pidgin English and fluent French of the regular inmates drift back to his pen. His SAS training kicked in. He kept up a rigorous exercise routine, even in the confined cell. On the day they moved him into the general prisoner stream he was ready for the expected move from the prison gang leaders. A team of four approached. He noted two were hard-muscled, the fitness freaks. The second duo carried nothing but attitude.*

*"We wanna give you a Maseru welcome, Mister Child Killer," one of the smaller men snarled. Boss Boy, leader, talker, won't do shit, thought Duval. Leave him 'til last. The larger heavies separated to pincer from either side, which suited him perfectly. He stared first at the gorilla to his right and beckoned him forward, pleased to see the momentary hesitation in his eyes. The man didn't move, and as Duval edged closer to him, he sensed the second brute pacing towards his back. In a sudden twist, he turned and met the on comer with a flying leap, landing his feet across each of the internee's knees and smashing his forehead full into his face, breaking the legs at the stiffened joints and knocking him senseless in one pass. The remaining guy did as expected, charging forward at Duval. His own weight and speed worked against him, as Duval thrust his heeled karate blow into his groin, then pulled the head down to meet his right knee. Twenty seconds gone, two attackers down. He moved towards Boss Boy, who backed off quickly, letting the third assailant come at him. The knife in his hand was easily dealt with. Duval sidestepped the*

*man's lunge, jerking his arm back sharply. The scream of pain told him the limb was broken. The dagger fell to the ground, but Boss Boy didn't move to pick it up. Duval swiftly retrieved the weapon. Then the guards stepped in, two with rifles pointing at his chest. The third guard, the senior man, Duval guessed, shouted, "Put that down or we'll shoot you, pig."*

*He did as ordered and waited, knowing this wouldn't be good. A rifle butt smashed into the side of his head and he lost consciousness. This saved him from immediate pain as the keepers kicked his body like an old football. Later he counted at least four broken ribs. His face was badly beaten, but surprisingly not to permanent disfigurement. The left leg bore the worst injuries, the knee completely damaged, where heavy boots had jumped on it more than once.*

*When he regained consciousness, Duval had no idea how long he'd been lying back in the solitary cell. His mouth was caked with blood and his tongue was swollen. The stiffness and aching in his chest told him the ribs were bad, but the leg pain was horrendous. What the hell had they done? No doctor came. No medication. Several days passed, with the scraping of the door opening to deliver food with water once a day. He dug deep. Deeper than he'd ever done. After what seemed like months, but was only a week and a half, they took him out of the jail to a clinic a mile away that customarily served the prison's medical needs. The doctor, who'd seen the brutal results of prisoner fights and civil war attacks over many years, told him he was lucky not to be dead. The ribs would heal, he said, but the knee needed surgery, unlikely to be available anytime soon. No gangrene, a blessing which meant in a week or two he'd be able to walk. Meanwhile, the medic gave him morphine shots to help with the severe pain in the joint and issued instructions to bring him twice weekly to the clinic.*

*"Why didn't they kill me when they brought me in? Why didn't they kill me in the prison yard? Why didn't they kill me in the privacy*

*of the solitary cell? Why? Why? Why?" he pondered. Then realisation dawned. "Of course! I'm the link to the killing. The tie-in to the bastard who ordered the hit on the bus. Their smoking gun – why there's no lawyer and no trial yet – why I get clinic treatment. It suits the bastards to keep me this way for now. Jeez."*

*Over the next few weeks, the knee continued to heal, and they allowed him into the yard twice a day to exercise, noticeably with no other prisoners. They didn't want him talking to anybody about the bombing. Clever bastards.*

*At six weeks, his leg had strengthened, but he feigned otherwise. He figured the clinic held his ticket out of there. It proved a lot easier than he'd imagined. The two guards who brought him on the weekly visit spent most of the time smoking outside the surgery. Alone with the doctor, a knockout blow to the back of the neck ensured at least twenty minutes before recovery and alarm. Unseen, he eased out of the side window and walked a few streets into the town, his getaway complete with the theft of an old truck. With no money and no passport, the airport wasn't an option. He took the best part of five days to negotiate his way across the border into South Africa, then drove to Durban on the coast. When night fell in the city, a couple of muggings provided some cash, his victims unaware that if there had been any physical resistance, they would have ended up with broken necks. The port-side bar area yielded a cargo coaster needing extra labour with no questions asked, done over a drink with a Dutch skipper. The voyage helped in getting his muscles back into shape. Ten weeks after the bus explosions, Rikko Duval stepped over the doorstep of his villa in Casablanca.*

*He used the sea passage for some hard thinking and solved a puzzle. If he'd been kept alive at the prison as living evidence of the bombing, that wasn't under instruction from the politician's rival. The order had come from the politician himself. The bastard had arranged the killing of his own daughter and the other kids to pin blame on his political opponent. What kind of animal behaved that way?*

*The Hotel Warrabi in Lagos is as five-star as any the city boasted. The visiting Lesotho Minister for Foreign Trade could sleep easy with his bodyguards posted outside the suite. The deal concluded in late afternoon with his Nigerian counterpart would be well received back home, and his cut, directed to a private bank account in the Cayman Islands, was enough to make this a good payday. He draped his jacket over the rear of the couch and poured a large slug of Scotch from the minibar. As he moved across the room, he picked up the remote control for the television and pointed towards the console. The green 'on' button clicked. A split-second later an enormous double blast engulfed the place. The bodyguards kicked in the door and met the devastation around the mangled body of their charge. No human being, not even a powerful, corrupt Minister for Foreign Trade, could have survived the twin explosions, front and back, the same technique that had resulted in the death he'd ordered of his own daughter exactly a year and a month earlier.*

Once more, the memory of the payback seven years ago brought a sense of satisfaction. Rikko Duval swallowed another painkiller and, smiling to himself, settled back to regain some sleep.

# CHAPTER 13

The grainy images shot from a lens a few hundred metres distant showed the unmistakable features of Manuel Estrada. The photograph sequence detailed a medium-height, stocky Caucasian shaking hands with the Mexican drug boss before stepping into a limousine with darkened windows. A second man held the door for the Caucasian and took the passenger seat next to the driver. The Drug Enforcement Administration agents tracked the vehicle to Boston's Logan International airport, where two other men met the target. They had 'bodyguard' written all over them. The group made its way to the check-in for Delta Air Lines and through passport control to the First-Class lounge. The DEA surveillance team discreetly showed their badges to the check-in clerk. Mister Clem Darcy and his travelling companions were booked to Istanbul. Darcy was one of Ahmed Fadi's aliases.

Ten hours later, the wired alert to Turkey triggered arrangements to tail the party north from Istanbul airport to a secluded private compound in the Black Sea coastal suburbs of Kilyos, the base for Fadi's business empire.

This information relayed back to Boston and appeared as an item of interest to all major law enforcement forces, including the Metropolitan Police in London.

Alan Rennie received dozens of alerts like these on a daily basis, but few carried the Istanbul connection. The report sounded bells in his head. Istanbul had been the starting point for the seized drug shipment on *The Constellation*. The link with Manuel Estrada was compelling. The

Assistant Commissioner sent a return message to the DEA and Interpol, tagging the possible overlap connection. He also gave Jules Townsend a call, with the same information. William Lang wasn't on his circulation list.

* * *

The CCTV footage from the car park in Berlin covered the period from a week before the shooting of ISP's head accountant. Through Donnie Mullen's connections with the local Chief of Police, copies of the film from eight of the cameras reached Jules and the team in London. For two days, hour after hour they screened the tapes repeatedly against the bare, white wall in the boardroom. Jules had the initial run-through with all the squad present, then re-runs in pairs looking at them. Jack and Malky first, followed by the two former cops, Paul and Donnie, finishing with himself and May-Ling, before having the six together again for another viewing.

"What've we got? Jack, you kick us off," said Jules, directing the debriefing process.

"The van shows up for two consecutive days before the hit," said Jack. "The plate number's as clear as crystal, so we know it's the same vehicle. Confirmed as stolen, as expected. It drives in about an hour before normal office closing time and exits minutes after she leaves in her Volkswagen. Identical timing both days. Standard reconnaissance stuff."

"On the afternoon o' the shooting they came earlier," Malky cut in. "About an hour and a half. They prob'ly wanted to make sure they'd enough lead time to get a parking slot close to her car. After they shot her, they didn't speed away. The gun silencer meant no triggered alarms, so no need to raise attention by driving too fast leaving the place. Yer men there've done their homework."

"Paul, Donnie, you guys get anything?" asked Jules, turning towards their end of the table. Donnie gestured to his pal to go ahead.

"Yes, we've some views of the occupants through the windscreen. The side windows are darkened, so the front shots are the only ones directly of their faces, sort of blurry. We had them enhanced and sent across to our mates at the Met to run the computer match checks."

"And?"

"So far nothing back. That's all we got boss. Not much. How about you guys?"

"Show them," said Jules, making way for May-Ling to play the tape showing the shooting. She located the sequence and set it in slow motion. The frames jerked across the office wall. The range was too close for the bullets to miss their target, and the ISP men winced as their employee's demise replayed. The light in the van switched on as the slide-door drew back for the shooter to do his work, the side view of his head illuminated. The shots matched the earlier pictures taken through the windscreen.

"The face doesn't give us anything new," said Jack.

"No, but this does. Look," said Jules, motioning again to May-Ling.

She played back a few stills and froze the reel where the gunman reached out towards his victim.

"There. Enlarge that."

The magnifier ballooned the image to six times the original. In clear definition, the hand holding the pistol appeared thin and veiny. Across the skin on the wrist above the thumb a distinctive birthmark spread like a large, coffee-spill stain.

"Good spot, Jules, you've got the eyes of a bluudy hawk," said Jack.

"Not me. The hawk eyes belong to your wife. May-Ling picked that one up. But I'll claim this one," said Jules, gesturing again to her. May-Ling changed the slides and ran the CCTV pickup from the bomb attack on the Moertens outlet. In a few seconds the frames moved to the assault on Martha Compton, the hammer blow to the store manager's head inflicted by the same bony hand bearing the unmistakable image of a large, coffee-spill stain.

"Bejeezus, Jules. You guys aren't human," said Malky, laughing. "So, we look for a bloke with a birth mark? All we've gotta do is to check the hands of three billion adult men and we've got 'em, right?"

"Not that," said Jules. "But it does confirm the New Bond Street hits are tied in with the murders of our own people." The mood quieted in the room. "Something else came in this morning from Alan Rennie."

Jules went on, "We never ever identified the lad whose shipment we busted last year. This guy keeps so low under the radar even Mac's records didn't surface anything for us. I think we might have an idea now of where and who he is."

They were all ears as Jules explained the intelligence surfaced via Boston and Istanbul.

"What do we do about it?" asked Paul.

"I've got some ideas, but I need to check out another couple of things before I bust your brains. Meantime, good work on this. I've already shared this with Alan at the Met."

As the meeting broke up, Jules said, "Malky, Jack, check your visas. We might be taking a little trip to Mexico."

Malky's expression spoke for him.

*Mexico?*

He knew Jules kept two or three moves ahead of most people, but this one he couldn't get immediately.

*Well, never mind. We've been here before wi' the boss, and I'm sure he knows what he's doin'.*

# CHAPTER 14

Cy Foster met Jules with a strong bear-hug. At six foot five, and two hundred and forty pounds of muscle, he towered above the ISP chief. The last time the pair had been together they led a combined undercover operation to eradicate a nest of renegade Honduran soldiers turned rogue killers, embedded in the jungle area of Mosquitia. The fire-fight lasted twelve minutes with total wipe out of the enemy for no loss.

Foster's handsome, African American features could have graced a movie set, including the diamond stud in his left ear lobe. His bass voice came all the way up from his toes as he greeted his visitors. A loose, faded-blue, denim shirt reached below his sweatpants, covering the holstered Glock pistol at his waist.

"Welcome to El Paso-Juarez, the DEA's little piece of Paradise. Hardly five-star, but hey, we do a mean line in coffee."

Jack and Malky shook hands with the head of station for the United States' busiest anti-narcotics field location. The converted warehouse nudged the Mexican border and was the largest of seven one-storey buildings in a fortified complex housing that Cy and several dozen operatives, all hand-picked. The open-plan space contained desks in clusters of six in the middle of the expanse, laden with telephones and wide-screen computers. Large-scale maps, with coloured circles indicating known border-crossings covered the warehouse walls, interspersed with groups of photographs pinned in columns showing different gang members. Many of the mug shots had thin red 'X's: confirmed victims of turf warfare or killed by the authorities. Others bore green, full-picture question marks – missing, believed executed. The war against the cartels was relentless, matched by the constant flow of drugs through dozens of relay points between the countries.

Cy leaned forward with his elbows on the desk, coffee mug smothered in his cupped fingers.

"What's cookin', Jules? You said you needed background stuff on Manuel Estrada."

"A long story, but the short version is we think he might've found a new friend in Europe. You ever hear of a guy called Ahmed Fadi?"

"Sure. He's the biggest mover and shaker of this shit all the way from Afghanistan to your backyard in England, right? Isn't he the ultimate invisible man? Must be shellin' out a fortune in payoffs to stay that way."

"We helped put a major spanner in his works last year. You probably heard about the raid on his boat in England. He's bound to be hurting for cash flow. A tie-up with somebody like Estrada makes a lot of business sense."

"You guys got a piece of that action?" Cy raised his eyebrows. "Nice work."

"Your people in Boston photographed Estrada looking cosy with an unknown Caucasian, traced back to Istanbul. Our betting says that was Fadi."

"And you've put two and two together to make five, right?" Cy said. "Why are you so interested in him? Last time I looked, you guys ain't law enforcement. What's the deal?"

Jules nodded to Jack to explain.

"Three of our clients were hit in the New Bond Street bombing heists," said the Scotsman. "Now the insurance companies want us to help get their gear back."

"You still ain't tellin' me why Estrada," said Cy.

"I'm getting there, big fella," said Jack, holding his hands up in mock surrender.

"A couple of days after the robberies, three of our people were murdered, two in Hong Kong and one in Berlin. We know there's a tie-in."

"Yer bastards took them out in cold blood," said Malky, the emotion still running strong with the Irishman. "I could understan' if they wanted a pop at us boys, but these were yer normal, innocent employees, for God's sake."

Cy nodded. "Personal, huh? I still don't get why Estrada. Jules?"

"There's more than one way to trap a rat," said Jules. "Going after Fadi might be difficult but could be done with a little planning. If we took him out it wouldn't halt the machine. The drugs would still get peddled. His supply lines and connections being smacked makes a more powerful impact. Not likely to stop the business forever, but recovery from that kind of damage would take months, not days or weeks."

"Fadi doesn't source from here, not from Estrada nor any of the other cartels. Where's this leadin' us?" quizzed Cy.

"His feeders carry the stuff in from Afghanistan, Pakistan and the Near East, fragmented, hundreds of routes," said Jules. "Difficult, but not impossible to disrupt but it would take time, a lot of time."

He paused and handed his coffee mug to Jack for a refill.

"Put yourself in Fadi's mind. He's thinking a tie-up with Estrada guarantees bulk supply, coupled with the cash flow from fencing the gems he's knocked off, his business gets secured. The value he lost he makes back in what, a year, eighteen months?"

The DEA man's face cracked in a wide grin. "Son of a gun. You wanna hit his new supply before he even starts, right?"

"Not exactly *before* he starts."

"I'm intrigued. Do tell," said Cy, a huge smile creasing his face.

"My guess is they'll run a trial shipment from here to Europe," said Jules. "Probably sooner than later. I suggest we let the stuff through, track them until it's under Fadi's control, then hit hard."

Cy roared. "Jules, you're a fuckin' genius. I like this. I like this a whole bundle, man."

Malky and Jack joined in the laughter. Kindred spirits don't take long to bond, and in Cy Foster they had one of their own.

Jules let the noise settle and said, "I've a couple of ideas to bounce off you."

"Try me."

"Okay. Estrada's cartel's not the only game here. These mobs seem to spend a lot of time shooting each other up."

"Darn right. Just look at the mug shots on the walls," said Cy. "Most of the red crosses are gang murders. Pity they don't go a hundred percent. Would do a big part of our job for us. Where you leadin' me with this?"

"You're keyed in to when and where these gangs transport stuff. It'd be good to try to funnel Estrada's actions in the next week or so. If you feel like sharing some of your intelligence on what you think's moving soon, a few interventions from us could stir the pot nicely. We only hit Estrada's competition, leaving him untouched. That does a couple of things. The competing gangs'll raise the heat on him as they'll think he's directing you guys towards them."

"What's the other thing?"

"The increased local pressure might speed up his move to ship out to Fadi."

Cy slapped the desk with a huge palm and roared again, his broad grin beaming at Jules.

"Man, it's a good job you're on the side of the good guys," he said. "I'd hate to be chasin' you down with a devious mind like that."

"You know this patch better than anybody. Do you think it's workable?"

"Oh, it's workable, more so havin' your team here," said Cy, waving his arm at Jack and Malky. "Maybe we can do a bit of damage together."

His huge fingers tapped at his computer keyboard. In a few seconds, a succession of pages danced across the screen.

"Here, look," he ordered. The ISP men did as they were told, standing in a semi-circle around the big man.

"We continually trace the major players. They follow patterns until we break 'em up. Then they come again, usually repeatin' the same routines.

With only so many ways they can get their shit into the States, they try land-crossin's, boats and planes. After the 9/11 attacks, security checks intensified everywhere, and public means of transit became off-limits. They're still tight."

"I guess they've built an entirely new network to move their gear," said Jack.

"Yeah. We've a whole screed of paid informants on the ground, some are useless, just takin' free dollars from Uncle Sam. A few feed us good stuff on a regular basis. A lot of penny-ante smugglin', too small to bother us, but the streamers, as we call 'em, we track daily. Here's what's fresh as of this mornin'."

A series of bullet points in bold characters appeared, with names, locations, and expected drug movements with allocated timings, some with different colours.

"Why aren't they shaded the same?" asked Jack. "Each gang colour-coded?"

"Yep," said Cy, hitting the keyboard. "Here's what you really wanna see."

A succession of photographs with the faces of known dealers tagged to their gang associations appeared on the screen.

"Accordin' to our sources, these boys are gonna be active this week. Three different mobs, three lots of movements, one tonight, and the other two tomorrow after midnight. These pictures are middlemen. For a cut of the action, they ferry the shit from one location to the next. Payment used to be in cash, and sometimes still is, but more and more they're takin' their cut in heroin and meta. That spreads the distribution even deeper."

"What about yer suppliers?" said Malky. "Where do they fit in?"

"They get the stuff from overseas, mainly Colombia and Peru, package 'em up in street parcels, and pass 'em along to the middle guys."

"So, the cartel men and the transporters are together at the hand-over points, right, Cy?" said Jules, stroking his chin. "And money changes hands at the same time?"

"Right on point one. A shipment hand-over will have at least half a dozen people from each side. Nobody trusts anybody. Lots of guns.

Somebody sneezes the wrong way, it can get bloody. On point two, as I said, it's not always done on a dollar basis. Depends on the players. Sometimes it's on consignment, but only for long-established dealers. Given who's involved tonight, the gig will be against cash. Tomorrow, one cash deal, one consignment. My teams are geared to hit all of them."

"Do any of these three belong to Estrada?" asked Jules.

"The first one tomorrow night's his people."

"How about we let that one go, and take down the other two? We can join you?"

"Easily done," said the DEA chief. "I'll get word out Estrada's gettin' a free ride."

Jack laughed and punched him in the shoulder. "You catch on fast for a big mother, don't you?"

"Easy enough for me to unnerstan' Jules here, cuz he speaks the Queen's English, but I've gotta lissen louder to unnerstan' the accents you and the Irishman spout," he said, returning the punch before Jack could move.

"Let's go meet my team and get you up to speed on the deal tonight."

The trio followed Cy towards the corner of the warehouse to join a group of four men and two female officers. Five hours later they were fully primed for the evening's action.

# CHAPTER 15

A good hairdresser costs money, one of the few indulgences May-Ling allowed herself. With Jack and the others away in South America, an appointment at her favourite salon in the Regency Hotel was fixed for ten o'clock. The valet-parking attendant handed her a number tag, before taking the wheel of the black Range Rover. The reserved parking on the ground floor ensured guests a minimal wait to retrieve their vehicles on departure. The attendant reversed the car in alongside a yellow Ferrari and a pick-up truck and walked back to his station at the front of the hotel.

Minutes later, a man carrying a small canvas bag appeared from the opposite side of the parking area and made his way to the rear of the Range Rover. He knelt down and removed a package from the sack. In a simple operation, he taped the payload under the chassis. As he stood up, another driver some bays distant accidentally pressed his horn in a sharp burst of noise, causing the man to look up.

*Nothing to do with him.*

He walked to the side exit and left as he had come, unnoticed.

May-Ling rode the elevator to the second-floor level, arriving ten minutes early at Cutaways. The receptionist greeted her warmly.

"Good morning, Mrs. Calder. I'm afraid your stylist called in a little late, something to do with a delay in taking her daughter to school. She'll be here in about half an hour. If you like we can have someone else look after you?"

"No, that's okay. I've an easy schedule today. I'll wait for her."

"Some jasmine tea as usual, then?"

"Yes, thanks," said May-Ling, making herself comfortable on the waiting-area sofa. She picked a couple of glossy magazines from the rack and settled in to browse the latest gossip from the world of show business. It never occurred to May-Ling her own life and career was as unreal to most people as those she read about in these magazines. The half-hour delay stretched to forty minutes before the arrival of her stylist, out of breath from racing to make up lost time.

"Mrs. Calder, I'm so sorry. My timetable this morning went completely haywire," she said. "First, the kid spilled her breakfast juice all down her school clothes. Had to be changed, then the car wouldn't start. I managed to flag a taxi after ten minutes waving my arms at a whole fleet of them. The cabbie waited at the school until I got her inside then brought me here, a nice guy. Cost a bloody fortune, though. I had to speak to the teacher of course to apologise for being late. Mama's fault, not my daughter's. You know the kind of thing, huh?"

"It's not a problem. We all have mornings like that. My day's free anyway, so relax."

"Thanks. You're an angel. Let's get your hair rinsed," she said, guiding her client to her work booth. "The usual works?"

Close to midday, May-Ling tipped the stylist, and left Cutaways. She rummaged in her handbag for the valet ticket as she walked toward the elevator bank. A few steps later the building rocked to a huge bang. She recognised it immediately as a bomb explosion.

*Here? In the hotel? What the hell?*

Then a cold wave gripped her.

*Oh, my God. The Range Rover! Could it be?*

Next to the severely damaged yellow Ferrari and the pick-up truck, the Range Rover had been transformed into a twisted mangle of steel and rubber. It was clear to the bomb squad officers the target was May-Ling's car. The device had channelled the blast up through the base of the chassis, propelling the vehicle high enough to hit the concrete ceiling. The handiwork of an expert, the strike would have killed any occupants, probably leaving them unrecognisable. By good fortune the parking level was deserted when the timer went off.

May-ling's life had been spared by the stylist's daughter's spilled breakfast juice.

* * *

DCI Bob Granger arrived at the car park where William Lang huddled in deep conversation with the hotel general manager and the security officer. He approached the group in time to overhear the chief of the Anti-Terrorist squad address them.

"Mrs. May-Ling Calder? The wife of Jack Calder of ISP? What was she doing here?"

"Good morning, William," said Granger. "I heard Jack Calder's name. How's he involved in this?"

"His wife's Range Rover's the blast source," said Lang, with no formal greeting to the DCI.

"Good job she wasn't in it when this thing blew, or we'd be picking bits of her off the roof. She's in the GM's office with my lads, helping our inquiries. Your ISP friends turned up pretty sharpish in New Bond Street, and when the missus nearly gets blown to kingdom come, they're nowhere to be seen. What d'you think's going on here, eh?"

The ice in Lang's voice was unmistakable.

"I don't know any more than you do," said Granger, indicating towards the hotel entrance. "Let's go find out if May-Ling has any insights."

Lang nodded to the general manager to lead them from the wrecked cars through the side passage connecting the hotel.

"The security guy tells me CCTV covers the car park," said Lang. "I've asked for the tapes, and you'll get a copy too. I suggest you tell your boss we need to nail this stuff quickly. The Minister's bugging me on this already."

Typical, thought Granger. Pass the crap on to Alan Rennie and keep any kudos for himself. Let's get this back on course. This is a police crime scene investigation, not Lang's playground.

* * *

A former policewoman, May-Ling knew the drill. Her interviewers were skilled in downloading information. Information covering everything about the intended victim. Herself. Her movements, not only today, but yesterday and as far back in recent days as she could tell them. Anything the slightest bit out of the ordinary she'd noticed? Her habits? Regularity in visiting the hairdresser? Movements sequence this morning? The mundane questions. Anyone with a reason to harm you?

Are they kidding? Pick any one of a dozen.

The hotel bustled with police. Detective interviews with guests present in the lobby when the explosion went off yielded little information. Likewise, with those in the rooms overlooking the car park. The parking team and foyer staff reported no unusual activity. The valet who drove the Range Rover remembered nothing out of the ordinary.

* * *

In the general manager's room, two of Bob Granger's men sat with May-Ling, together with a pair from the bomb squad. Contrary to Lang's earlier comment about her *being with my lads, helping our inquiries,* the Met officers were in charge of the interview.

"Hello, May-Ling. You okay?" asked the DCI as they entered the room. She raised her hand in a relaxed gesture and shrugged her shoulders.

"This is William Lang, head of the Anti-Terrorist team," said Granger. "Bad business, this."

"Good afternoon, Mrs. Calder," said Lang. "I'm sure this attempt on your life is unnerving, but we're here to help you. Please try to give us as much detail as possible. May I ask why your husband's not here?"

Bob Granger picked up on May-Ling's irked body language. In three sentences, Lang had managed to be patronising, condescending and rude, a talent not missed by his interviewee, the least likely person in the room to be unnerved.

"Mister Lang, my husband is currently overseas on business, but I'm quite capable of looking after myself, thank you. Your colleagues already questioned me at length. They should be able to give you my detailed feedback with great clarity. I don't think I've missed anything. I'd like to leave now, if you don't mind. My day's screwed to hell and the fallout from this'll take me a while to sort out."

"I'd prefer you to stay a little longer and go through it one more time with me," said Lang. "Sometimes these boys miss things, you know?"

May-Ling stood and picked up her bag.

"No, Mister Lang. I don't know. Perhaps you should do your homework. I used to be in the force too. I know how to conduct interviews and these boys, as you call them, did a terrific job of it. Unless you feel you want to arrest me, I'm leaving."

Lang stepped aside to let her sweep from the manager's office.

The suppressed smirk on the DCI's face matched the elation he felt.

*That told the bastard! Jack Calder's wife's got more balls than Lang'll ever have.*

# CHAPTER 16

The briefing finished at five-thirty in the afternoon, with the move-out scheduled at eleven p.m. Including Cy, the combined attack force for the evening now numbered eight men and two female officers. For the next two operations, they would dispense with the customary DEA insignia on the armoured vests. From current information, they expected a dozen or more gang members at the first hand-over rendezvous.

The new additions to the task force checked their M16s in rotation. Jack to Malky, Malky to Jules, and back to the Scot, in a pass-the-parcel process. The machine-pistols received the same treatment. The DEA team followed their own preparation drills but weren't as precise as the ISP men, their chief noted.

*Always something to learn from other pros.*

At nine o'clock, Jules asked Cy to repeat the proposed action plan.

*Detail, detail, detail.*

Each of Foster's squad took turns to walk through parts of the sequence. Jules nodded his satisfaction at the seamless way they covered their business.

The night-vision binoculars picked up the movement of small unlit trucks converging on the target site. Six vehicles, with a higher headcount than anticipated. The ISP men each partnered with separate DEA groupings. Jack buddied with Cy and one of the female agents a hundred metres from the entrance to a yard surrounded by an eight-foot wooden fence. A two-storey private residence sat forty metres back from the opening. The property belonged to a known drug trader but had been unoccupied for several months.

*Kinda stupid having just one way in and the same way out*, Jack thought.

Situated at two further vantage points, the other groups waited for the signal from Cy.

The front four approaching trucks entered the compound in procession, only feet apart. A few minutes later, the last two drove in behind them. Previous experience told the watchers the middle pair would be carrying the merchandise. The last two held the buyers. The wooden gates swung shut. The DEA chief counted down from ten then spoke into his radio.

"Time to party, ladies and gents. Go! Go! Go!"

The female agent gunned the armoured jeep toward the gate, crashing into it at speed, with the remaining two jeeps tight behind them. The wooden spars offered no opposition as they sped into the yard and screeched to a halt. The second DEA squad entered the compound and the last blocked the exit. Jack followed Cy out of the vehicle, both with M16s primed.

"Get your hands up," the big man roared. The men inside had opened the back doors to the vehicles holding the drug load. The panicked reaction of reaching for their weapons proved fatal for some. In seconds, half a dozen fell lifeless to the ground. Others with enough split-second reasoning dropped their guns. The assault team moved in with caution, covering those left standing. From the corner of his eye, Jack caught sight of an armed figure at the second-storey window pointing toward them. "Incoming! Upstairs!" he yelled. Both he and Jules blasted the silhouette at the same time. The glass shattered and the bullet-riddled corpse of the guard tumbled down to the yard. One of the gang on the ground took the diversion as a signal to reach down for his weapon. He died before touching it.

Four of the DEA team entered the house and in a five-minute sweep ensured no remaining resistance lurked inside. In minutes, the attackers secured the ten prisoners in the yard with plastic-wire handcuffs and bundled them into the captured trucks.

"You're as slick as ever, Cy," said Jules, patting his pal on the shoulder.

"Hey, I shoulda had the upstairs window covered. Good job ol' Jack's eyes work. There's a good haul here, I reckon 'bout three million bucks worth. Now watch this," he said.

Cy called one of the captives over to him, a young man who looked in his teens.

"How old are you, boy?"

There was no reply. The big man slapped him across the face, drawing blood from his lip.

"Don't fuck with me, boy. How old are you?"

"Fifteen. And fuck you too," came the snarling reply.

"If you wanna live to sixteen, get the fuck outa this game, y'here?"

He beckoned to one of his men to unlock the cuffs.

"You're too young to fuck your life up with this shit. Get outta here. And tell your friends not to screw around in Manuel Estrada's patch. You got that?"

The DEA agent led the boy to the gate and threw him out. The lad turned and spat on the ground before sprinting into the darkness.

"Very clever, Mister Foster. Very neat. Now the message gets back as sure as hell," said Jules.

"Yeah, normally these kids are full-blown criminals by his age, but lettin' him carry the word is okay. We'll prob'ly pick him up again in a coupla weeks."

"How about the bodies?"

"We leave 'em here. Uncle Sam ain't gonna pick up the burial tabs, and it's a nice callin' card for the rest of 'em to see," said Cy. "Let's get back and grab some sleep, we've another gig in twenty-four hours."

The convoy, including the seized trucks and their cargo, eased its way out of the compound and back toward the DEA base.

* * *

The teenager relayed the message.

"Sí, Señor, the big black guy says to stay off Manuel Estrada's patch."

"Did these hombres have DEA vests?"

"No, Señor, but the guy sounded Yankee. My boss is dead now. Can I work for you?"

Estrada nodded. "Sí, you did well. You can come work with us. Here, this is for you. Go find a bunk."

He picked a few hundred-dollar bills from a roll in his hand. The boy took the money and left the gang leader wondering why the hell, and who the hell would think Manuel Estrada's business needed protection? Everybody knew the biggest and most powerful cartel operator had plenty of guns of his own. Why use Yankees? Anyway, he had a shipment to take delivery of tonight. Better ensure a bit more protection, just in case this stunt triggers a backlash.

* * *

"Yes, Jack, I'm a hundred per cent okay. Relax."

May-Ling replied to her husband's question for at least the fifth time during the phone call. Jules and Malky listened to Jack's end of the conversation with some consternation. The personal threat was escalating faster than predicted. Jules signalled Jack to give him the line when he'd finished talking with his wife.

"I'm glad you're not hurt," said the boss. "Go over this again for me, as slowly as you like."

"Sure." She, like the men under Jules, knew how thorough he needed to be. A couple of re-tellings of her version of events didn't take long.

"By the way, William Lang's probably doing his job, but he knows how to get a lady's back up. The guy's a pain in the ass, big time, Jules."

"We'll deal with him through Alan Rennie. Did you ask for the hotel CCTV tape copies?"

"Bob Granger's promised we'll have copies by the time you guys get back."

"Okay. I don't think our offices are prime targets now, but all the same, reinforce the red alerts. We'll be back in London the day after tomorrow. See you then."

# CHAPTER 17

"Word of last night got back for sure," said Cy. "Our insider called. They've moved the meet and I expect they'll be gunned up more than usual tonight."

"We still hit them?" Jack asked.

"Yeah. But I wanna work our timin' a bit different. We're told they're gonna switch to the night-market on the south side of town. Out in the open air."

"Ordinary Joe Public with his wife and kids'll all be there?"

"This mob's not dumb. They reckon nobody'll smack 'em in a place like that."

"We don't go in blasting with innocent people in the line of fire, right?" said Jules.

"Correct. But as you've said before, there's more than one way to trap a rat. Here's how we do it," said Cy, spreading the city street map across the campaign table. Similar to the previous day, the team absorbed the detail and repeated back in sequence. Everyone had a designated function. Everyone had a specific back-up buddy. Everyone knew the fall-back plan and then a third option in case of need.

The night-market arena covered no more than three acres of scrub-ground. Every square inch crammed with stalls peddling anything and everything from children's clothing to fruit and vegetables. Toys, games, and books. Trinketry, home-made and imported. Live animals for slaughter on the spot, and various contraband items flushed into the market, stolen or diverted from goods delivery shipments in the city. An endless supply of fast foods cooked on gas-fired cylinders fed the nightly hordes of customers. Traders' whole families from grandparents to babies scattered among the makeshift barrows and stands. Their livelihood depended on working contributions from everyone.

The handover could be at any point inside the complex, ruling out the possibility of hitting the gang without endangering innocent bystanders. The main entrances, one from the north-west corner, the other from midway along the east of the area, made observation simpler. Wait and watch.

Cy added two more agents to the squad and split them into six pairs. Impounded vehicles from previous raids served as transport. Unmarked, unidentifiable, easy to blend in with the traffic flows. Three units each scattered along the two approach roads. Battle dress of casual clothing gave no hint of the impact power in each small convoy. From the parked positions, all movement in and out of the market had to pass them. Jack partnered with Pammy, one of the female agents, and Malky with Cy in the convoy covering the north-west. Jules buddied with one of the men in the other pack guarding the east approach road.

The earpiece crackled in Jack's ear.

"We have movement. Two cars, two vans, nose to tail. They're our game. Stand by," said Cy. "Just keep watching, team."

"Copy that," came the response from the lead car on the east perimeter. "We also have one closed van and three other vehicles coming in convoy. Looks like a lot of head count. Over."

"Copy. Expect them to hand over fast and head out fast. Tail and intercept as planned. Over."

Five minutes ticked by. Then eight. The earpieces crackled again.

From the east. "Movement. All four vehicles exiting in close order. Picking up speed."

"Follow and intercept at your own timin'," Cy's instruction resonated. "No way yet of tellin' which lot has the shit aboard. We also have a convoy comin' at us this end. Go, team, go!"

The rapid intercept from the east squad, with Jules included, worked like clockwork. A blocking pincer from the two lead DEA cars brought the fleeing gang skidding to a disorganised halt. A ring of high-powered weaponry took out the front car's tyres and met no resistance. No guns appeared from this group, signalling the drugs were in the other mob's possession. Smooth, easy arrests.

A deadlier sequence played out at the north-west corner.

The speed of the getaway indicated the value of the cargo aboard. Cy barked into his mouthpiece.

"Hit 'em."

The trio of intercepting pairs slammed the accelerators in the same pincer cut-off movement. Cy in the right-hand scissor, Jack in the left. The third team cut into the rear blocking position. Jack and Cy both unleashed volleys at the tyres, ripping them to shreds. Unlike the other interception, an instant response of firepower from all four of the gang's vehicles ripped into the DEA squad's convoy. The windscreen of Jack's car exploded as a line of fire thudded through into the inside of the roof. The bullets whined on the way past his head. He spun out of the car and lobbed a stun grenade over the first car at his side. The detonation rocked both the front cars of the mobsters. Aware that Cy was doing the same on the opposite side, Jack aimed his AK47 upward into the nearest target. He heard simultaneous gunfire from across the debris. Then silence. The shootout lasted only thirty-three seconds. Screams from two of the gang's ravaged cars meant some were still alive. Jack turned back to his own vehicle to check on his female buddy. He froze. The staring eyes and blood-smeared forehead told its own story. The line of bullets missing Jack had found a victim.

A voice called from the rear team.

"Zak's dead."

Another DEA member killed. Cy appeared beside Jack and saw the dead woman.

"Oh, no," the big man whispered. He moved forward and gently felt for a pulse at her neck, only to confirm the obvious. Cy's arms tensed, the fists clenched in controlled rage. The icy grip that had seized Jack's gut and left him momentarily paralysed, returned in force. The mind-numbing fear the dead woman could one day be May-Ling. He had known the same thing in Northern Ireland at the death of children hardly old enough to go to school; in Central Africa, at headless mutilated corpses from horrific ethnic cleansing; and the same with the civilian slaughter in the Balkans many years ago. The same fear, he understood, often kept him alive, conscious of his own mortality. SAS-trained or not, they were all only humans. Humans are vulnerable to bullets and grenades. The command from the DEA chief brought him back to the present.

"Find me one of these bastards still breathin', and somebody make sure Pammy here's looked after properly."

Four of the drug gang were alive, one in urgent need of an ambulance. Cy was in no hurry to provide one. He used the same technique as in the hit from the previous day. He chose the youngest survivor, a teenager scared out of his wits, unlike the hard-nosed kid from the other gang and sent him packing with the message, "Mister Estrada don't welcome no interference from no upstart outfits."

The haul was low-grade heroin, but a lot of it, with street value close to USD700,000. Another good night's work.

The two killed agents were irreplaceable.

# CHAPTER 18

The unmistakable image of the face on the CCTV film from the hotel car park confirmed the link to the atrocities in New Bond Street.

"Some noise startled him, possibly a car horn, causing him to look up," said Alan Rennie. The Assistant Commissioner had commandeered the copy tapes himself, and together with DCI Bob Granger brought them to ISP's offices. William Lang was conspicuously absent, uninvited.

"Recognise the guy?"

"We certainly do. That's Rikko Duval," said Jules. Around the table sat Jack, May-Ling and Malky.

The flight back from El Paso-Juarez had dragged for the Scotsman. The tightness in his stomach over concerns about his wife subsided only when he reached home. Before the front door had closed, he grabbed her to him in an embrace tighter than she had ever known from him. May-Ling had felt the release of tension in his chest and arms. She understood his anxiety and spent the best part of the morning repeating she was okay and telling him to stop worrying. Even now, Malky noted his buddy sat closer than usual to her, his elbow balanced on the back of the chair, but with his hand touching her shoulder.

"Any idea where a guy like this might be?" asked Alan.

"Not a clue. We weren't even sure he was still alive, but while he is, he could appear anywhere. No use looking for him as Duval," said Jules. "He'll have a string of aliases. Unlikely to have any close friends. Nothing to pick him out. Just as likely to be sipping coffee on a beach hut in Brazil or raising chickens in the bush in Australia."

Malky cut in. "Yer man's about as invisible as ye'll get. The money he picks up for these contracts means he can go quietly where he wants, when he wants. Wi' that limpy leg o' his, yer not gonna see him goin' too public anywhere."

"Malky's right," said Jack. "His clients contact people like him through the underworld grapevine. Even then, there's never a direct link. Like having cut-off drop boxes. Sometimes there's as many as four or five links to get to one of them. Deniable at each level. Instead of trying to find him, we should be looking for things leading to him, such as the money he gets paid. Find out where it's getting paid, and who's doing the paying."

"Hey. I'm the cop here," said Rennie, joking. "You guys are going all detective on me." He pushed his coffee cup away and leaned on the table. "But you're right. The question is, where to start?"

"Can I make a suggestion or two?" said May-Ling. Jules nodded.

"We've only got bits and pieces to run with, none of which points to the big boys," she said, stepping up to the chalkboard.

She wrote the headings, 'Duval', 'Fadi', and 'Estrada' across the top, then below these, the next line, 'Cash', 'Jewellery', and 'Drugs'.

Jules smiled and leaned back in his chair, clasping his hands behind his head.

"Go on," he said.

"In Chinese we say, 'the fly leads to the fish, the fish leads to the man'. Any one of these in the second line might get us to at least one of the names on the top. We know already Fadi and Estrada are linked. Estrada is the 'Drugs', Fadi is the 'Drugs' plus the 'Jewels', Duval and Fadi are both the 'Money'. Alan, your friends at Interpol have resources to trace large payments from Fadi's companies' accounts. That might get us a handle on Duval's whereabouts. From what I gather from the activity in El Paso-Juarez, the drugs shipments will help us to Fadi, and perhaps to Estrada at the same time. What do you think, Jules?" she said, glancing across the room to her boss.

Jules turned to Jack and joked, "I've told you before, it's amazing how all the brains in one family stay with just one person. May-Ling's with the programme already. She's right. Alan, can you get your tracers onto the bank payments, and maybe some lead-back from the stones offered in Istanbul? One more thing. It might be advisable at this stage if William Lang's not aware of where this is going."

"Agreed," said Rennie. "You're scanning abroad with this. Nothing under local jurisdiction to warrant troubling Lang. I'll tap my pal at Interpol and advise you if we find anything useful. I'll also send this photo of Duval through to Interpol. We might get lucky. Anything else?"

"I think that's all for the moment. Thanks Alan."

The Assistant Commissioner left. Jules stared at the chalkboard.

*It might just as well have been a chessboard*, thought Malky.

* * *

The strong personal bond between Alan Rennie and Marcel Benoit, Head of Interpol in Lyons, sprung from a twenty-five year, crime-fighting liaison across Europe. Each man understood when to manipulate the legal rules and when not. The telephone conversation moved swiftly from their routine greetings to the reason for Rennie's call.

"Our drugs boss in Istanbul may possess a face at last," said the Assistant Commissioner. "Jules Townsend and his team have a professional and personal interest in the bombings in London, and it seems they've surfaced a connection to Istanbul, a guy called Ahmed Fadi."

"Tell me," said Marcel.

"Some interesting pictures were snapped in Boston with another of your international targets, Manuel Estrada."

"Now you're talking, my friend. Big fish swimming together? What interests these gentlemen to be engaged with each other? They operate in completely different markets. I'm not aware of any previous hint of collaboration."

"Jules has a notion that Fadi's loss last year prompted the hits in New Bond Street. Your pals in the DEA have been making Estrada's life uncomfortable for several months. Circumstance can throw together some unexpected bedfellows."

"I wouldn't question for a moment any theory Jules arrives at, Alan. The man oozes great instinct. How can I help?"

"Another name's trickling out. Rikko Duval. Former SAS officer, turned bad. An explosives genius and possibly a killer for hire. I'll fill you in later on all the reasons, but Jules thinks this Fadi might have contracted Duval for the Semtex work in London. He also tried to kill May-Ling Calder."

"Ouch," said Marcel. "That *is* personal. I wouldn't like to be Monsieur Duval running up against the ISP boys."

"I agree. Thought is one thing. However, proof is quite another. Duval is invisible. There's no clue where he is, or where he sleeps, nothing. We're not certain if he *is* alive, but if it's not him, we're left with no leads whatsoever. I'm prepared to run with Jules' theory for the meantime. One train of thought says Fadi paid him a stack of money. Your access to bank account tracking will be helpful."

"I hear you. I'll sniff around. You know it's not easy dealing with the police on the ground in Turkey. Too much bribery. This will take some time, my friend."

"I understand, Marcel, thanks. I'll catch up again soon. G'bye."

Benoit finished the call and redialled. The instructions he issued to his agents were clear and simple. Find out everything available on Ahmed Fadi, his companies, his cash flows. Don't use the Istanbul police contacts. Get Interpol's local narks involved. He replaced the phone and mused on what kind of hornet's nest this elusive Duval had stirred up by attacking Jack Calder's wife.

# CHAPTER 19

Nothing remains private for long in the El Paso-Juarez underworld. The grapevine was on fire for days after the hits on his rivals with news Manuel Estrada had acquired some heavy-duty, foreign protection. Subtle and not so subdued murmurings surfaced, including planted newspaper snippets pointing to Estrada and his people having done a deal with the wrong devil. At the same time, Cy Foster's team continued to hit the smaller feeders for the Mexican's operations. The opposition from the other gangs was of no concern, but the added pressure from the authorities served to hasten the plan of action agreed with Ahmed Fadi. Within days, the DEA informant relayed the shipment details. The American Government's grease dollars still spoke volumes. Date, cargo, shipping route, transit pickup points and final destination, all buttoned down.

Cy issued instructions to cover the El Paso end of the process without physical intervention. This was one load he wanted to see make it all the way to Europe.

* * *

"They're takin' the long way round, Jules," drawled Cy. "Down to Dakar in Senegal and trans-shipment up to Turkey. The handover's gonna be in the south-western seaport of Antalya on or around ten days from now for on-shipment to Istanbul. The designated transit handover point on land is the port's dockin' bay area number five."

"Great work, my friend. That's some information network you're running."

"Bonus information for you. The merchandise'll be picked up by a security truck from Tri-Square Security, comin' all the way down from Istanbul. Tyin' in kinda neat. What's the bettin' Tri-square belongs to Ahmed Fadi?"

"Brilliant, Cy."

"I'd expect the truck won't be travellin' solo. My gen says there's three million bucks' worth of street shit in that cargo."

"Perfect. We'll start planning now. If you hear anything further let me know."

"You got it. Keep me informed the other way. I wanna know what you and the crazy Irish-Scots duo are doin' on this one."

"Deal. Thanks again, Cy."

The international call had been relayed on the speaker. Jack and Malky were all smiles as their chief terminated the conversation.

"We've got some homework to do," said Jules. "Let's get the ordinance maps for Antalya. We'll need the layout of the port and any info on security."

*Detail, detail, detail.*

# CHAPTER 20

The London bank's Head of Security asked the safe custody vault officer to go over his story a few times. After the fifth visit by the men with the Moroccan leather case, the nagging in his head had become too strong, it was time to alert his superiors.

"Just a gut feeling, sir. Prob'ly all above board. Just something I can't put my finger on. Thought I'd better mention to you."

"You did right. Let me think about it. Give me a heads-up when they visit again, okay?"

"Will do, chief."

The officer left the room. The security boss leaned back in his chair, hands clasped behind his head, looking at the ceiling, running through all the information he'd just been given. Several minutes later, he dialled the direct number of his mate, Assistant Commissioner of Police, Alan Rennie.

"You know we're not supposed to do profiling like this, don't you?" said the police chief, in more of a statement than a question. "It does seem a bit sniffy. You're aware of the stuff we've been chasing down for the past couple of weeks, Bertie?"

"Precisely why I called you, Alan," said the security honcho. "Did you know we hold back-up copies on all clients' keys for use in emergencies? I'm not permitted to go snooping on the bank's clients, especially not in the custody vault area. However, if I'm presented with a legitimate police search warrant, what's a guy to do, eh?"

Alan Rennie roared with laughter. "Let's say this is a preliminary peek inside. Do you think myself and Bob Granger could drop by for a wee look? If anything shows, I promise I'll get you a back-dated warrant. No need to mess everyone around with paperwork if it comes up blank?"

"Sounds good to me. Come in tomorrow morning at seven, before opening hours. Just myself and the vault officer'll be here. And bring some croissants."

The pastries were still warm in the takeaway bakery bag as Alan Rennie handed them over to his pal.

"Enjoy your breakfast, Bertie. Thank Bob here, he paid for them," he said with a grin.

"Didn't expect a bloody Scotsman to pay for them anyway," said the security chief, picking the larger of the two croissants and handing the other to his vault clerk. "Let's go down to the custody room. We can eat on the way."

The controlled lift access to the basement level two floors below opened into a well-lit area. The Assistant Commissioner acknowledged Bertie's pointed finger toward a series of CCTV cameras along the ceiling, covering every square inch of the ante-room to the custodial space, but none inside the walk-in vault precinct. Bertie's colleague motioned to the ranks of chrome-fronted doors of the safety boxes, each with twinned keyholes. He turned the key in a large box two rows from the top. Bertie followed suit with the master key. Inside the box, crammed rolls of black cloth left little room for anything else.

"May I?" asked Bob Granger. Bertie nodded and the DCI removed the topmost roll and placed it on the table adjoining the back wall. The thick twine binding the cloth took a few moments to undo. As the contents of the package were revealed, Alan Rennie whistled.

"Well, I'll be damned. Jackpot, Bertie. Bloody jackpot."

Accentuated by the blackness of the cloth wrapping, several diamond-mounted pieces of jewellery sparkled in the bright illumination of the vault.

"Camera, Bob. Snap these and we'll get them compared with the stuff that went walkabout."

The vault clerk re-wrapped the items, taking care to ensure the revelation wouldn't be noticeable when the box owners came to reclaim them.

"You said they've another two boxes," said Rennie. "Let's open them, please."

The second cache was already partially empty, but the third was as full as the first. Bob Granger repeated the camera work.

The vault clerk locked the barred doors behind them as the quartet returned to Bertie's office.

"The official search warrant will be with you before noon today, Bertie," said the Assistant Commissioner. "In the meantime, we'll want the addresses on these opening account forms. The backroom lads'll follow up on these, but I wouldn't expect them to yield much, but who knows? Bob, I want you to coordinate with Bertie. Arrange a twenty-four hour, invisible watch until these guys come to open any of the boxes again. Check the photographs to make sure we're not kidding ourselves here. If these aren't from New Bond Street, I'm a Dutch uncle. If it *is* the stash from the heists, I want whoever comes back for them arrested. Post a couple of plain-clothes boys with Bertie until further notice. Let's get back to the office; we've got a bit of work ahead of us this morning."

"Guess you owe us another bag of croissants, Alan," said Bertie, grinning from ear to ear, as he shook hands in parting with the police officers.

The addresses on the bank opening account forms showed three separate corporate names. Contrary to Alan Rennie's expectations, they reaped a valuable harvest. All three carried the same building, same floor address in London's West End. A quick site visit from a local detective showed the names shared a brass-plated signage with several other company names, under a banner group, East-West Trading. A follow up search at the Companies Registrar of the group's base led back to Istanbul. A confidential call to Marcel Benoit requested a discreet enquiry on the ownership without alerting the local Turkish officials. The Assistant Commissioner specifically asked Marcel to sniff around for any links to the Ahmed Fadi group. His gut instinct was in overdrive. Now it was waiting time again.

# CHAPTER 21

Late afternoon drifted into early evening in the ISP boardroom. Used coffee mugs and sandwiches cluttered the centre of the worktable. The walls carried magnified street maps of the area around the port in Antalya, lifted from ordinance survey sheets only a couple of years old. Coloured markings highlighted the principal focal points. Around the table, Jules, Donnie, May-Ling and Jack faced the wall as Malky went through the summary.

"Yer main entrance and exit to the docks have no gates but the individual loadin' sheds are secured front and back. The one Cy gave us the heads-up on, number five's got slidin' doors at the front, and swing-openers at the back, here." He tapped the sheet with a huge finger. "Yeez'll notice it's the last bay, closest to the road system out o' the place. The feedback says it's got the quietest traffic area of goods in and out. Owned by one group. No prizes for guessing whose?"

Jules nodded. "East-West Trading. Go on. Overall security manpower at the port?"

"Minimal," said Malky. "Blue-collar guards. A couple o' roamin' jeeps, more for show than anythin' else."

Donnie spoke from the end of the table. "What's the deal with Customs people? Antalya's a port of entry."

"Marcel's reports say they're as bribe-laden as anywhere in the country," said May-Ling. "I'd guess when this shipment arrives, there'll be no holdup for transfer to the shed."

"Which also means, probably fewer eyes around," said Jack. "If customs boys've been paid off, they won't want to be in the vicinity in case it comes back to bite them. No see, no do, no blame, Right?"

"Correct, my man," said Malky. "But let's not take anythin' for granted."

"Okay," said Jules, ticking off some headings on a pad in front of him. "Run us through the timings again."

"Right, ye are. The boat's supposed to arrive from Dakar mid-evenin' the day after tomorrow. It'll be dark outside the port, but inside, the flood lightin'll still be on. They might lower the lights around shed five, but maybe not."

Jules wrote something on his pad as Malky talked.

"We'd be daft to presume the shed guards won't be armed, and heavy-duty gear into the bargain," Malky continued. "No way o' tellin' how much o' a reception committee to expect."

"That won't matter too much. I'm sure they won't be expecting visitors," said Jack. "Speaking of visitors, what the hell are you doing here?"

The door to the boardroom had swung open and the large frame of the DEA chief for El Paso-Juarez stepped in.

"Hi guys," the voice boomed, and the usual huge smile lit his face. "You mean you didn't tell them I'm comin' along, Jules?"

The ISP boss rose to greet his pal with their customary hug.

"Take a seat. No, I thought better to wait for you to turn up," said Jules.

He addressed the squad. "Cy insisted he join the party, and since we enjoyed his hospitality last time around, how could I say no? Besides, somebody has to carry the calling cards, eh?"

Greetings were exchanged all round, including with May-Ling, the first time she'd met the big man.

"I can see why you were in such a hurry to get back home, Jack," said Cy, the grin growing even wider. "Nice to know you at last, May-Ling."

"Malky, let's run through this again now our interloper's here," said Jules, settling back into his chair.

The Irishman recast the summary up to the point of Cy's entrance. Jack stood up and approached the wall to continue.

"Interpol people will meet us at Antalya airport. We're flying in via Paphos in Cyprus, private flight, courtesy of Marcel, the same evening the goods are expected to reach the sheds. There's two hours turnaround time on the ground before flying back, but the port is only about fifteen kilometres away. Gives us plenty of time to do what we need to do. We've asked for a couple of local pick-up trucks. That should attract no attention when we drive onto the dockside. The hunting party is Malky, Donnie, myself, and now, it seems, our gate-crasher as well."

"You ain't comin' Jules?" said Cy.

"Too many cooks spoil the broth," said Jules. "You four are plenty for this hit."

"The locals supplyin' the hardware too, I s'pose?"

"Yes. M16s, stun grenades and laser pistols," said Jack. "We make the hit, disappear back to the airport, hand over the vehicles and weapons and get aboard for the return flight. The Interpol guys will be on standby in case the timing changes. Right now, from what they can track from Senegal, everything's on schedule."

"Any questions?" said Jules, rising from the chair.

Shakes of the heads all round showed no need for elaboration.

"Well, a bit of news from Marcel this afternoon. His cyber-intel system has traced some large payments from Ahmed Fadi's outfit into a bank in Gibraltar. While you're flying from London to Cyprus tomorrow morning, he and one of his lads are paying a courtesy call on the general manager at Reliance Bank. I'd like to be a fly on the wall for that one. Okay, dinner, anybody? We've got to show Mister Foster a bit of British hospitality."

The ops meeting closed with murmurs of approval and smiles at Cy.

# CHAPTER 22

"I'm afraid I can't help you, Inspector. Without a police warrant, I'm not permitted to disclose details of any of my clients' business to unauthorised persons or agencies. Rules are rules."

The smug look on the face of the general manager of Reliance Bank displayed his annoyance at police intrusion on his fiefdom.

"I'd rather hoped we could do this like gentlemen," said Marcel Benoit. "Of course, you're correct. If I have to *force* your cooperation, I need to have with me formal warrants."

The banker's smile persisted.

"Which is why, Monsieur," continued the Interpol chief, "my colleague here brought a warrant, not for the specific account I was hoping you'd help me with, but for every account in this office."

Marcel's companion agent produced a thick envelope from his briefcase, as the smirk died on the banker's lips.

"We've reason to believe Reliance Bank may be engaged in wholesale money laundering, which if proved to be the case will involve serious criminal charges against any and all senior officers in your institution, not least yourself, Monsieur."

The General Manager sat down and stared at the unopened envelope on his desk.

"There must be some mistake. This bank is clean," he said.

The arrogance switched in seconds to startled confusion. The bead of perspiration on the bridge of his nose and the nervous, clenched fists gave Marcel his opening.

"Our suspicions may well be groundless, but you do understand while any investigation proceeded you would be obliged to close the bank for whatever time it may take us. Days, possibly weeks, who knows? However, Monsieur, I much prefer to deal reasonably with our friends in the financial world."

"Tell me again what you need to review, Inspector. Perhaps I was a bit over-formal in my reaction. We at Reliance Bank wish to maintain good relations with the authorities at all times."

"Thank you. I think this envelope can remain sealed for the meantime," said Marcel, handing it back to the agent. "I've no desire to disrupt the bank's business, nor indeed at this point to freeze the account to be discussed. The account is in the name of Robert Cavendish."

"Mister Cavendish? Inspector, he's the largest single depositor in this bank. The behaviour on his account has always been impeccable. He holds large investments in blue chip companies. We regard him as an excellent High Net Worth client. The bank operates with strict rules on account management. Mister Cavendish has never stepped outside of these parameters. Regular communications are made to his email address, and he visits us from time to time."

"Is this your client?" Marcel placed on the desk a copy of the file photograph Mac had given to Jules.

"Yes. Several years younger, but unmistakable."

"You keep an address for Mister Cavendish? Telephone contact numbers?"

"We use a normal poste restante arrangement in-house for his bank mail, Inspector. Mister Cavendish travels extensively. We arranged for an original Post Office Box address for him in Geneva, which is a common feature of many of our High Net Worth clients, but his instructions are never to send mail. He collects as and when he visits us."

"How often is that?"

"He called in about a month ago, I remember, but he has no set pattern."

"Mobile or landline telephone numbers?"

"Mister Cavendish utilises a French mobile number, but only as a backup for text messages if we have a problem with the email communications."

"Do you ever contact it?"

"Only once I can recall, something prevented an email getting to his inbox. The message bounced and we re-sent by text to the mobile number. He did receive that as he later got back to us by email."

"Monsieur, you will please give me details of the email address and the mobile telephone number. Under no circumstances are you to share any of this conversation with your staff, and most certainly not with Robert Cavendish. Be assured Interpol has means to detect if you breach these instructions. In which case, not only will the warrant we discussed earlier be rigorously enforced but you personally will be liable to arrest for collusion in a criminal enterprise. Do you understand?"

Marcel glared at the general manager.

"As I've said, Inspector, we will cooperate with you at all times. May I ask what kind of criminal activity Mister Cavendish is suspected of?"

"You may not. For your own safety, better you are privy to nothing more than we've covered this afternoon. Furthermore, if continued activity occurs on the account or should he visit this office again, you will deal with him as normal, but call me direct on this number," said Marcel, handing over his Interpol business card bearing his name and direct private telephone number.

Ten minutes later, the Interpol chief and his agent left the bank. The folded paper tucked into his inside pocket carried the requested contact details.

"It's amazing how the fear for one's own skin instantly overrides the interests of the institution that's fed a man for years," said Marcel, following his colleague into their car. "Anyway, we've something to trace now. Get a check on the triangulation on the mobile phone. If the SIM card's still in place, that'll narrow down the area. Also instruct the technical guys to track where the emails end up. I'd be surprised if the phone is live, and the email terminal won't lead to a computer or laptop where Duval lives. More likely to be an anonymous internet café routing, but it might help to focus in on the locale."

Marcel made a few notes on the short plane trip back to Lyon, marshalling his thoughts to be shared later with Alan Rennie and Jules Townsend.

# CHAPTER 23

At another bank in London, police work and patience were playing out well.

The vault officer opened the security box for his visitors and returned to his post. The pre-coded call to his boss patched through immediately.

"They're here, sir. Just gone into the vault."

His chief gave the nod to DCI Bob Granger and his three-man team in the lounge. No other clients were in the basement, as per policy. The arrival of the policemen in the vault area coincided with the men leaving. The cameras captured the attempt by the taller client to swing his attaché case at Granger's head. The blow parried upward as he caught his arm and spun the man around, pinning him against the wall. A second detective applied the handcuffs. The other man's headlong dive to evade capture ended with a rough body tackle.

The detectives read them their rights. Bob Granger instructed Bertie, the security boss, to seal and date-stamp the CCTV film covering the last two hours in the vault. Indisputable evidence showing pre-entry to the area, the signatures on the box number and handling the stolen merchandise it contained would be unassailable in a courtroom.

The case held jewellery identifiable as stolen from New Bond Street.

* * *

Five hours after the arrests in London, Ahmed Fadi received word his operations in England had hit a severe snag. Two of his top lieutenants were under lock and key, no doubt bearing intense interrogation from the Metropolitan Police.

The captured men would reveal nothing. They valued the lives of their families. Of more significant importance to the crime lord were the impounded packages of jewellery from the bank's vaults. Hundreds of millions of dollars' worth. The cash flow pile.

Fadi's Balkans reputation for coolness as a guerrilla commander belied a ferocious temper. He seldom made a decision in anger. His initial rage subsided as he regained control of his emotions, mulling over the course of action needed now.

An hour later, he called Rikko Duval.

* * *

Fadi's assumption was correct, as Alan Rennie and William Lang tussled for seniority in managing the case. The head of Anti-Terrorism would not be as easy to divert this time as at the hotel bombing interview. The two men discussed the issue in Rennie's office. The Assistant Commissioner had ensured Bob Granger joined him for the meeting.

"We'll take over jurisdiction, Alan," said Lang. With these arrests, he had something at last to appease the Home Office Minister.

"I don't think that'll be necessary, William. For the moment, the chain of evidence merely involves possession of stolen property."

"These men are liable to terrorism charges, which take precedence over any possession nonsense, my dear fellow."

"On the evidence as it stands, there's nothing to justify a terrorism charge supportable in a court of law. Not in my opinion," said the Assistant Commissioner. "My experience tells me if we press anything other than those I've stated already, a sharp lawyer'll throw the book at us, and we'll be left with nothing. Besides, my detectives made the arrests and logging of the evidence trail. Standard procedure, William, the case stays here meantime."

"Perhaps a word from someone above us both can clarify this, don't you think?" said Lang. Bob Granger knew the condescension in Lang's voice riled Alan Rennie but his boss kept his cool.

"I'd be glad to take direction from any proper authority senior to us both, William. Meantime if you need anything else from me, I'm always pleased to be of help," said Alan. The response carried an unspoken message to the Home Office man.

*You've no seniority over me and if you want to try pulling rank, go ahead. Right now, I win.*

Granger watched, not for the first time, an outwitted head of Anti-Terrorism leave empty-handed.

# CHAPTER 24

William Lang's secretary explained the caller would only speak to the decision maker in charge of the bombings' investigation.

"Who is this?" he asked, when the connection came through.

"It doesn't matter who I am. Listen carefully. I won't repeat myself. I'm sure your tracers are tracking this call, so I'll be brief," said the voice. "The key to your bombers lies with Jules Townsend and May-Ling Calder. King's Cross Station. Left luggage locker number 218. Across from platform seven, near the tea-shop. Ask them what it means."

"But what do they have…" The dial tone went dead.

Rikko Duval tossed the mobile phone into the nearest wastepaper basket. A single-use purchase. Maybe one of the best investments he'd ever made. Time would tell.

A career politician in the making, William Lang cared nothing for the subordinates he worked with on his way up the political pecking order. A brighter than average student, his talents stretched no further than an ability to reproduce facts during school examinations. The man's personal initiative centred solely on selfish objectives. The family boasted upper middle-class pretentions. His father spent a lifetime in local government in a mid-level position, with a credo bred more on surviving in the system than surfacing, the overriding mantra being not to make mistakes. Uncle Herbert had prospered better, rising to Private Secretary to a State Minister who held three posts over a period of many years. Herbert's connections were influential in fast-tracking the younger Lang into his current position as head of Anti-Terrorism. The bombings in New Bond Street offered the first public test of his mettle. He needed a positive development to claim success. The timing of the anonymous telephone call could help deliver a win for him.

The flush of excitement waned as Lang tried to make sense of the call. First the arrest of the men at the bank two days ago, and now this. Something to peddle with his superiors. In Lang's view, that obnoxious bastard, the Assistant Commissioner, would have to be sorted out one day. In the meantime, he had to wait for the information flow from Rennie's desk on progress with the arrested men. According to the Scot, so far, interrogation of the Eastern Europeans had yielded nothing of any consequence. They carried no identification, hadn't asked for legal representation, and answered none of the barrage of questions thrown at them. The wall-clock showed a touch after six. Chances were, the ISP people would still be in the office. He collected his jacket and instructed his secretary to have the car and driver stand by. A short drive across to the West End offices of ISP unannounced would leave Townsend and Mrs Calder no excuse to avoid him.

His luck held.

"Good evening, Mister Lang," said Jules when the agency chief appeared at his office door. "To what do we owe this pleasure?"

"Forgive my not pre-announcing myself, Mister Townsend. I received an interesting phone call a short while ago and wanted to come to discuss it with yourself and Mrs Calder. Is she here also?"

"Yes, I'm here," said May-Ling, arriving at the office door. Both she and Jules donned their professional veneer, disguising their inherent dislike for Lang.

"Thank you both," he said, taking a seat opposite Jules. May-Ling chose to sit nearer the wall, a little distant from the men.

"So, tell me about your telephone call, Mister Lang," said Jules.

Ten minutes elapsed during which Jules asked William Lang to repeat himself a few times.

"We know nothing of this," said Jules, nodding at May-Ling. "I think you're dealing with a prank call. What do you intend to do now?"

"Would you mind accompanying me to King's Cross? Perhaps we can clear this up quickly?"

From the corner of his eye, Jules saw May-Ling roll her eyes toward the ceiling. This man was a nuisance, but a persistent nuisance. Jules decided to close this down as soon as possible.

"Okay, we'll come and check it out. We'll take our own vehicle and meet you at King's Cross in about half an hour."

"Thank you. I knew you'd understand the need to follow every lead on this."

William Lang missed the sarcastic flourish of May-Ling's hand as she waved him out of the office.

# CHAPTER 25

Lang's departure from the meeting with Jules and May-Ling coincided with an arrival involving ISP personnel half a continent away.

The private flight from Cyprus landed two hours ahead of London time. Security clearance wasn't needed. The Interpol agents handed over the keys to a pair of nondescript vans. In the rear of each, a broad cloth covered the weapons and blackened night-gear for the assault. Jack and Cy took the first vehicle, Malky and Donnie the other. The pairs spent five minutes double-checking the weaponry before heading out toward Antalya's port area.

The route covered no more than twenty minutes of driving in light traffic. No vehicles cluttered the dockside's main eastern entrance. The squat hangar for bay five stood twenty metres back from the wide driveway. One half of the large front shutter door hung ajar. Outside, two men sat on a wooden crate, smoking. Jack and Malky slowed as they drove past, taking in as much as the limited view would yield without causing more than a cursory look from the guards. A hundred metres later, Jack turned the vehicle around and waved to the others. Take-down time.

The vans sped forward and braked in unison in front of the smokers. Cy and Donnie exited first and pointed their guns at the men. Jack and Malky followed suit with no words and little sound. Donnie gestured with his weapon for the pair to move inside the shed. Half a dozen other men spread around inside. They all carried guns. One of the smokers screamed a warning and flung himself to the ground. It was the last act of his life.

The firefight lasted seconds. The intruding quartet dropped to one knee and fanned the shed with deadly fire. Three of the men inside died in the first salvo. The others were injured, one fatally, two were still alive.

Cy kicked the gun away from the feet of one of the survivors and pulled him into a sitting position. He put his pistol to the man's head.

"If you wanna keep breathin' you show me where tonight's delivery shipment is."

"Go fuck yourself," came the reply. The man sneered and turned his head. The shot from the pistol blew his brains away. Cy walked to the other injured guard. No persuasion was needed this time.

"There. Over there," he said, pointing to a small tarpaulin on a steel rack at the side of the shed.

"Nice line in questioning you have there, big man," said Jack using his knife to slice through the first package to reveal the dun-coloured raw cocaine. Jack nodded. Donnie stepped forward and fixed a couple of detonators to the stack.

"The third guy didn't make it," said Cy. "That leaves my squawker here as the only messenger. Ain't this his lucky day?" He lifted the injured man and carried him to the door of the shed.

"Listen up, buddy. You tell your boss this. Friends of Mister Estrada don't like him doin' business with you amateurs. You got that?" The guard nodded. Cy pulled him ten metres clear of the building and joined Jack in the van. As the vehicles drove out of the port, the detonators did their job.

Fire engine sirens screeched in the opposite direction, passing them on the way back to the airport.

# CHAPTER 26

The station's rush-hour foot traffic had thinned. William Lang stood opposite the left luggage lockers beside a gentleman in uniform. Jules and May-Ling approached, and Lang introduced the man.

"This is the deputy stationmaster. He holds the master keys for the lockers. We can solve this in minutes. Shall we?"

The four walked toward the bank of boxes. The railway man led the way with the key in his hand, Lang and Jules a metre behind him. A few metres back, May-Ling checked her watch. Jack and the team would be preparing for action in Turkey. The station officer tried the lock. Nothing moved.

"It's jammed," he said. The brass key protruded at a slight angle from the lock, stuck tight.

"Let me try," said Lang taking hold of the offending key.

Something instinctively triggered in Jules' head.

"No! Don't touch it!" he called.

Too late to heed the call, the Anti-Terrorism chief yanked at the key.

The deafening explosion reverberated around the station.

* * *

Donnie Mullen took Paul Manning's call on his mobile phone as they waited to board the plane in Paphos for the connecting flight back to England. Jack saw his partner stiffen. He heard Donnie say his wife's name and an icy grip of dread flowed from his neck to his toes.

"What's up? What's wrong?"

"Bad news, guys. Really bad news."

"Spill it. What is it?" asked Jack.

"That was Paul. Jules and May-Ling were caught in a bomb attack at the left luggage lockers in Kings Cross Station. Lang was there too. Jules and Lang are dead. May-Ling's in hospital. One of the station staff was also killed and a dozen other people injured."

"What the fuck? How badly injured is she?"

"Serious, mate. She was unconscious when the ambulance took her away, and she hasn't come to yet. Paul's at the hospital now."

"What the fuck were they doin' at Kings Cross?" asked Malky. "And wi' that asshole, Lang? Jules dead? Fuckin' unbelievable."

"Paul's got no idea what they were doing there," said Donnie. "He said Jules was killed outright. So was Lang."

Cy gripped Jack's shoulder. "I'm sorry, man, really sorry. Looks to me like a classic booby trap."

"Rikko Duval. Bastard. Bastard," Jack whispered.

It would be a long flight back to London.

# CHAPTER 27

The intensive-care staff moved silently and efficiently about their duties. Paul stood up from his chair in the corridor as his three ISP partners and Cy strode toward him.

"The doctor's in there with her now," said Paul, nudging the door open and speaking softly to someone inside. In moments, the specialist appeared and reckoned Jack as the husband by the strained look on his face.

"How is she?"

"Mister Calder? I'm Doctor Spencer. Your wife regained consciousness for a little while earlier, but we decided to induce a controlled coma." The soft-spoken medical man addressed the assembled visitors with total authority. "She suffered severe blast trauma on most of her left side. The two men in front shielded her from the worst of the explosion, but she's in a serious condition. We've stabilised her vital functions for the moment. The next twelve hours are critical. Rest assured she'll get the best medical help we can provide."

"Her injuries?" asked Jack, his mouth stuck dry.

"It's touch and go whether or not she'll lose her left eye, but if we save it, she's unlikely to have full vision in it. Her shoulder blade is broken, and she's suffered typical blast trauma on her left arm and leg. These we can sort over time."

"Can I see her now?"

"For a few minutes only, please. She's not conscious. Oh, and by the way, I think the baby will be okay."

"Baby? What baby?"

"I'm sorry. I thought you knew already. Your wife is eight or nine weeks pregnant, Mister Calder."

Jack stared at each of his partners in turn, his mind reeling. His *pregnant* wife in an induced coma?

A nurse appeared from the room and the doctor spoke to her, "Nurse, can you get a gown for Mister Calder. He may go in, but for a little while only, please."

The numbness in his body made everything move in slow motion. The nurse held the door open for him. The others waited grim-faced in the corridor.

Two more nurses attended the bedside, one monitoring a bank of equipment with several wires attached to the body on the bed. May-Ling. His wife. Mother of their first son, already at University in Edinburgh. Mother-to-be of another baby. If she lives.

Her head was heavily bandaged, the left eye completely covered. The bedclothes were not tucked in. Draped across the bed, a light sheet hid the web of wires from the machines. He caught the powerful smell of antiseptic. A wave of nausea hit him. Hard. His head spun.

"May I sit down?"

One of the nurses took his arm and led him to the chair near the bed. That was better. He swallowed a couple of times. Clarity returned. He talked to himself, a trait he'd practiced over the years in some horrific situations.

*Get a grip of yourself, Calder. Jules is gone. Dead. Your wife's fighting for her life here. She's carrying your baby. Stop acting like a fucking chicken, man.*

A cool thermal wave of control eased back into his thinking. His brain clicking, checking, checking. May-Ling was in the only place that could help her right now. Nothing he could do or say could impact this. Time to get out and let these good people get on with their work. He rose abruptly.

"Thank you, ladies. I know you'll look after her for me."

He left the room with a quick glance back at the woman he cared more for than anything else in the world. This part was out of his hands now.

* * *

The international media channels covered the horrific pictures soon after the devastation at King's Cross. Bad news sells better than good news. Television interviewers pitched at vantage points with as much of the carnage in the backdrop as possible. Appalling scenes make more riveting viewing. Advertising hoardings in the station stood in tatters. Glass and wooden rims from windows punctured by the blast spread across the forecourt. Paramedics and nurses worked the makeshift triage tables. The only noise was the wailing of fire alarms nobody had switched off, mixed with the repeated public-tannoy message announcing the station was closed.

* * *

In Casablanca, the architect of the blast listened for any hint of responsibility for the deaths of three people and the dozens injured. The closure of the station caused horrendous traffic problems, which also consumed much of the coverage. Eventually, he heard what he was waiting for. A senior police officer addressed the cameras.

"At six fifty-five this evening an explosion at the left luggage locker area at King's Cross Station resulted in the deaths of William Lang, a senior member of the Anti-Terrorist Unit, Julian Townsend, chief executive of International Security Partners, and Melvin Crombie, deputy stationmaster. We would like to assure the travelling public everything is being done to curtail any further threat to public safety. We expect King's Cross Station to be closed at least until tomorrow afternoon, while the investigation into the cause of the explosion proceeds. Further information will be available as we have it ourselves."

Duval noted no specific mention was made of a bomb, as is standard practice. Regardless, the memory of the devastation in New Bond Street would be fresh in the public's mind. No word of May-Ling Calder.

Well, can't hit a home run every time, he thought.

* * *

A few hundred miles from Morocco, Ahmed Fadi's evening in Istanbul was filled with reactions to a compressed series of events. An hour after the ISP attack on Estrada's drug shipment, his temper raged as violently as his lieutenants had ever known. He cursed at the stupidity of his guards in Antalya, at the incompetence of the police security his bribe money financed, at the leakage which could only have come from that bastard Estrada's side, at the audacity of the mercenaries who had intruded on his business, in his backyard, in his fiefdom. As ever, the anger boiled only for a short time, to be replaced by partly blaming himself for not having monitored the movement of the drugs more personally.

Not long after the news of the fiasco in Antalya, the television newsreels restored a malevolent satisfaction as it became clear how effective Duval's hit had been in London. The streaming headlines repeated the names of the dead. None were of any interest to Fadi, except the former-SAS Major, Julian Townsend.

The private telephone purred and he picked up, expecting to hear his hit man on the other end. Instead, the unmistakable growl of Manuel Estrada greeted him.

No pleasantries preceded the vitriol as the Mexican launched into a tirade of insults and accusation.

"What the fuck went wrong with your people? Let's try out a nice, easy, safe shipment to start us off, you said. You would take care of everything on your side, you said. You've got the local guys on a fucking string, you said. And what happens? Your shitheads lose the whole fucking lot. You owe me, Ahmed. You owe me big time. How the fuck can I trust you with any of my business when you can't even babysit an easy piece of crap like this?"

No-one ever spoke to Ahmed Fadi in this way. The bile rose in his throat. He controlled his voice and spoke almost in a whisper. He used no curse words and erred on the edge of politeness.

"If you're quite finished with your little rant, Manuel," he said. "First of all, I would advise you never to speak to me like this again. Ever. Secondly, you should be aware of a message left with the only survivor from the attack this evening. It points to you and incompetence at your end being the reason for the hit in Antalya. One of the killers was a big, black, American guy. He mentioned your name twice. He said friends of yours don't like you doing business with me. I think there's something badly wrong with the way you run your own operation."

"You go fuck yourself," Estrada screamed down the line. "Don't dare tell me my operation's flawed. This shit happened on your ground, under your care, not mine. You'll pay for this one way or another."

The line went dead. Ahmed Fadi eased the receiver back onto its cradle. He had some hard thinking to do.

# CHAPTER 28

For over a thousand years, Winchester Cathedral welcomed into its cavernous high-vaulted place of worship the good and the great, the high and the mighty, nobility and commoner. Seldom was it ever as packed as the day of Jules Townsend's funeral service. The family home situated less than a mile and a half distant, but for his widow and children, it was the longest journey of their lives. The horrific injuries inflicted from the focused blast at King's Cross meant a closed casket, a mahogany, polished coffin, draped with the Union Jack colours. A neatly tucked beret sat on the flag, with the clearly-embossed emblem of the SAS pinned left front, the winged dagger and the words, 'Who Dares Wins'.

His widowed father, now a retired stockbroker, sat erect in the far front pew right, closest to the centre aisle, staring at the pedestal cradling his son's body. Alongside were his grandson and granddaughter. Jules was an only child, and the only other close relative, his widow, flanked the children. Jack and Malky had the two remaining places next to her.

Jack scanned the congregation. The left front pew filled with representatives from the highest ranks in Her Majesty's Armed Forces, including Mac from Stirling Lines barracks. The uniformed array included two princes of the realm in full dress uniform. In the public domain, little was known of the exploits and service given to his country by an outstanding commander of men. Within the echelons of secret operations, he was already a legend. Every other seat was filled, row upon row leading back from the altar. The mourners comprised local friends of the family and former classmates from Eton and the military college at Sandhurst, at which a young Jules Townsend had excelled in every aspect of his training. The vast majority of the rest of the space contained uniforms of various ranks from different military disciplines. Current and past members of the SAS made up almost one half of the attendees. Also prominent, senior personnel from other special services forces around the globe acknowledged the passing of a special one of their own.

Deputy Commissioner Alan Rennie and DCI Bob Granger nodded greetings from three rows behind. Next to them sat Donnie Mullen and Paul Manning. The large frames of Cy Foster and Marcel Benoit covered the remainder of the pew. Former Gurkha regiment officers had flown from Nepal to say goodbye to a man whose respect for them had been mutually returned. Jules Townsend had been a commander, a fighter, a strategist, a fellow combatant, and a man of honour and dignity.

All this, Jack Calder internalised. There would be no tears today. But another emotion roiled within him. Rage was not a common visitor to the Scotsman. Even in the horrors of lethal war situations over the years, he had followed his mentor's example. Anger leads to rashness. Rashness leads to error. Error leads to death. Today, as he watched the familiar grief dwell on the faces of Jules' widow and children, his loathing of Rikko Duval intensified. The final emphasis hit him as he caught the pain in Townsend senior's eyes. At that moment, he understood that he, Jack Calder, retired SAS officer, would never be the same person again. Revenge is a terrible emotion, both for the one seeking it, and for the one being targeted.

The report in the morning on May-Ling was encouraging, with the assurance his wife would live. The doctors as yet had no predictions regarding her eyesight and her mobility. Jack knew the combination of killing his best friend and the attack on the woman he loved could only be settled in one way. There in the front row of the cathedral he promised himself there would be a bloody and savage payback.

Strict orders from the highest level prevented any television coverage of the funeral inside the cathedral. Too many faces present required anonymity. The only visual permitted was a shot of the pallbearers carrying a hero's remains to the graveside. Jules was laid to rest beside his mother. The photograph carried across newspapers and news reports on the usual channels worldwide.

* * *

In El Paso-Juarez, Manuel Estrada stared at the picture. The big, black guy in the centre of the three pallbearers on the left side of the coffin triggered a thought.

*Son of a bitch. I wonder...*

He called his right-hand man. "Get that kid in here, the one who came to me after the takedown at the hacienda. The one the black hombre spoke to. Yeah. Now."

The boy held no fear as he appeared in front of the big boss. Estrada pointed to the newspaper on the desk.

"Is this the one who gave you the message for me?"

The boy peered at the paper for a few moments.

"Si, Señor Estrada. He's the one. For sure."

"How can you be so sure?"

"There, Señor. Look, the diamond stud in his ear. Besides, he's an ugly hombre too, no? Who could forget that face?"

The drug boss roared and slapped his leg.

"Ugly? Oh, yes, he's ugly alright. I think he's so ugly, he'd be better off dead." Another roar at his own humour.

"Okay, get back to work. Here."

He rolled off a couple of hundred-dollar bills and gave them to the boy. When the lad had gone, Estrada gave further instructions to his honcho.

"I've been thinking all along the hits must have been coming from the DEA bastards. Get this photo out on the streets. We need some reliable information on this hombre. His name, any word on his movements, anything. Then we'll prepare a present for him, no? Move."

The lieutenant left a thoughtful boss behind him as he summoned his own men to start the process of sniffing out information on the black dude.

# CHAPTER 29

Duval never drank alcohol, Fadi only seldom. Cigarettes and drugs were also off limits. Each respected the use of their own senses and faculties too much to risk having them dulled with unnecessary indulgences. Tonight, two days after Jules Townsend's funeral, a pot of fine Turkish coffee sat on the table between them, with ample finger-foods spread across its broad marble top. Fadi had dismissed his guards from the sitting room to their usual stations outside in the corridor, within calling distance. Fadi poured coffee for his visitor and handed the demi-tasse across to him.

"Your plan worked to perfection, my friend. Mister Townsend won't be troubling us anymore. It would appear Mister Calder's wife has also been removed."

"I'm surprised Townsend jumped in so easily. The man with him wasn't as careful as I expected Jules to be," said Duval.

Ahmed Fadi was unaware of his hitman's inner gloating. Rikko Duval had waited a long time to exact his revenge on the officer he blamed for ending his SAS career. "May-Ling Calder was a bonus, but she's not been reported dead. It depends how much of the detonation got to her. I watched her fall, and something tells me she's seriously wounded but not fatally."

"You watched her fall?" Fadi's incredulity showed in the rise in his voice. "You were in the station when the thing went off?"

"Of course. In the coffee shop opposite. If the reckless Mister Lang hadn't played with the key, I had a coded transmitter pointed at the locker, ready to blow when these guys closed in. If a job's worth doing, it's worth doing properly, Ahmed. Right?"

His paymaster locked eyes with the bomber. He saw no mirth, no delight, just a matter-of-fact executioner's gaze staring back at him. He nodded his head slowly and allowed himself a smile.

"How did you get out of there?"

"Easy. With all the mayhem and screaming, I just walked away. No-one gave me a second glance. The problem now is dealing with the rest of the guys from Townsend's shop. They won't know who's behind this but, you can bet your ass, they'll be pulling in favours all over the place to find out. My guess is you'll be high on their suspect roster, but they've no idea who you are, have they?"

"Me?"

"Not you by name, Ahmed, but they'll put two and two together and find a motive. That motive leads to whoever lost the drugs shipment last year."

"Yes. I thought of that already. My people they arrested in London won't talk. Everything here in Turkey is watertight and my personal security is assured."

Fadi refilled the coffee cups. Neither man knew they were both wrong. Rikko Duval and Ahmed Fadi were the only names under focus from Interpol, Alan Rennie, Cy Foster, and more dangerously, Jack Calder.

"You didn't ask me here to discuss the outcome in King's Cross," said Duval, switching the subject. "What's up?"

"Last week wasn't all successful," said Fadi.

"The hell it wasn't. You won't get a sweeter hit than that anywhere," said Duval.

"Oh, I don't mean Mister Townsend's demise. You won't have seen any newspaper reports on this, but the same night you were in London, professional assassins attacked one of my operations in the south. They murdered five of my men and destroyed a special cargo."

"Calder?"

"I'm certain."

"How come?"

"One of the hit squad was a big, black man. He left a message with the sole survivor to tell me not to deal with certain proposed new partners from overseas."

"So, where's the problem? You win some, you lose some. You plan to hit them back, including Calder? You want me in again?"

"All in good time, my friend. There's a more pressing matter."

"Tell me."

"The product destroyed belonged to the proposed new partner. He's going crazy. The man has no temperament for dealing with delicate situations. He called and spoke to me in a way I tolerate from nobody. I think he's foolish enough to try to act on his threats toward me."

"I understand. You want him taken care of?"

"Yes. And soon. I'm not concerned so much about him personally, but about what his loose talk might lead to."

"Where is he now?"

"He's based in El Paso-Juarez, on the border of Mexico and Texas. My intelligence tells me either the competition or the Yankee authorities have been scoring a few hits on his activities, maybe both. Either way, his security stinks. Can you handle it?"

"Sure. Everything is possible. It just takes a little bit of planning. He won't be expecting you to come after him, I suppose?"

"He doesn't think as straight as that. Arrogant bastard."

"Okay. Get me his details, including photographs. I'll need about a week. I want no contact either way until I'm finished."

Rikko Duval stood up to take leave of his client.

Ahmed Fadi would hardly have considered himself in those terms.

# CHAPTER 30

The watchers inside El Paso International Airport concentrated on flights originating from London. They didn't have long to wait for their quarry. A chain of four of Manuel Estrada's men tracked Cy Foster's exit from the plane, through to the waiting car at the kerbside. Walkie-talkie radio signals exchanged with the operational guys outside set other vehicles in motion. Traffic bunched close to the international exit road, slowing cars flowing toward the city centre. The laundry van veered across Cy's limo and slewed into the passenger side. In seconds, five other vehicles emptied a dozen men, all armed with high-velocity weapons. The head of the DEA in Texas and his two colleagues with him had no time to react. Round after round of bullets smashed through the windows and sides of their car. It was all over in less than twenty seconds. The killers took time to check the result of their work before leaving the scene. The three agents had no chance, their bodies hideously torn to shreds with the amount of incoming fire. It would be another two hours before Jack Calder received word his new-found buddy was dead.

On the same day, Rikko Duval's plane touched down in El Paso-Juarez. His business-class ticket permitted a complimentary limousine transfer to his hotel, but he preferred to use the airport taxi service. His usual hand-carried luggage needed no porter assistance. The less visual impact he left in his wake, the better. Porters and limo drivers tend to remember customers. The journey to Hotel Bravo absorbed half an hour.

The registration clerk barely glanced at the counterfeit passport as he paid for five days stay in advance with dollars. Duval knew some of those dollars would end up in the clerk's pocket.

With preparation to take care of in the following few days, the three-star accommodation suited his desire for low-key visibility.

* * *

The ever-present smell of antiseptic hung in May-Ling's room. Jack's second visit of the day coincided with the change in duty nurses, and he was already familiar with the earnest faces looking after his wife. During the earlier morning shift, she had regained consciousness enough to recognise him sitting beside the bed, his hand lightly touching hers.

He spoke gently. "Don't try to talk, sweetheart. Everything's gonna be okay." *What the hell else could he say?*

She blinked her eyes several times as he gazed at her face.

*How much had the bastard hurt his woman?*

She stared at him, and with a faint smile winked purposefully at him. His heart flipped.

*She's recognising me. She's able to think.*

Several minutes later, her eyes closed as sleep set in once more.

Now, ten hours later, she was awake again. Her eyes darted at him with concentration, communicating in her own way.

*God, he loved this woman so much.*

"Can you step outside for a little while, Mister Calder," said Doctor Spencer, arriving through the door. "Routine checks. I'll brief you as soon as we've finished."

"Of course, Doc, thanks," said Jack. He joined Malky in the corridor.

"How is she, big man?" asked his pal.

"She can't speak yet. But her brain's in good shape. I can tell by the way she's talking to me with her eyes."

"Grand," said Malky. "She's a warrior, that's what she is. But there's bad news from Mexico, Jack."

"Mexico? What news?"

"Cy Foster and two of his buddies were shot to pieces at the airport in El Paso. Didn't stand a snowball's chance in hell. The bastards ambushed his car and strolled away like some fuckin' Sunday School picnic."

"Fuck. First Jules and May-Ling. Cy wasn't part of ISP's plans in any of this. Why the fuck is he hit?"

"I think ye'll find yer drug man in El Paso had a few scores to settle with him."

Jack sat down beside the Irishman. Losing Cy was barely believable. Jules was dead. Two better expert special ops men than these would be hard to find. Both murdered in the space of a week.

"It's vendetta time for these guys, Malky. Whatever the reason for taking out Cy we can guess at. Our man in Turkey is tied in, for sure. And Duval's still invisible. Not good."

"What do ye propose we do?"

"We do what Jules would do. Never wait for dangerous assholes to come hunting you. Go find them and clean them out. Whatever it takes, Malky. We've friends in important places. Let's use them where we need. We get organised, and we execute." Jack stressed the last word with controlled venom. "You in?"

"Is the Pope a Catholic?"

They stood up as the private-ward door opened and Doctor Spencer joined them.

"Mister Calder, your wife's condition's still critical to serious, which is one level better than yesterday. She's a strong lady. Her vital signs are improving, and the baby is still in good shape. I can tell you from my last couple of examinations, she's suffered no brain damage. But this will be a slow progression."

"I'm grateful to you and your staff," said Jack. "Any estimate of how long she'll have to stay here?"

"At least a month or so, depending on her reaction to the medicines and therapy."

"Can she be moved?"

"Why would you want to move her? We've all the resources at this hospital to care for her recovery."

"To be blunt, Doctor, the people behind the bomb attack could want another bite at us and at her. I'm not sure we should be putting the hospital at risk. She needs heavy armed protection."

"Mister Calder, I had an excellent conversation with Assistant Commissioner Rennie earlier today."

"He was here today?"

"He's been here every day. Oh, I know his detectives must pursue their investigations as well as they can, but it's clear to me he's personally concerned about what's happening with your wife. He apprised me of the danger and possible further attempts on your wife's life. This is a private ward, and this wing is secluded from the rest of the hospital. I've already made clear to the Board of Trustees my patient will not be moved from here, and they agreed unanimously to allow armed protection. In fact, I think that's arriving now."

The sound of steps preceded the arrival of Bob Granger and three plainclothes officers. Jack exhaled a long breath of relief. Thank God for Alan Rennie and his lads.

"Hello, Jack, Malky," said the DCI, shaking hands with them. "My boys here will be on rotational shift every eight hours. She'll be safer here than anywhere else you can think of parking her, Jack. By the way, we heard about Cy Foster. Too bad, just too bad."

"You're right," said Jack. "If she's at home, it's too high a risk. Your guys'll do a great job. Thanks. Now, if you'll excuse me, I want to say goodnight to my wife, and then Malky and I have some work to do."

Jack entered the room and approached the bed. May-Ling was awake. He touched her hand. "I love you," he said. "You're the most precious thing in my life. Bob Granger's men are here. You'll be well protected," he said.

Her lips moved without sound as she mouthed the words, "I love you, too."

He made to leave, and her mouth moved silently again, "Get him, Jack. Get him."

# CHAPTER 31

His explosives expertise would serve him little in El Paso-Juarez. The fall-back planning required more time. Rikko Duval needed information and a weapon.

The local television channel in his room carried the news of the murders of the DEA operatives at the airport earlier in the day. Reports assumed drug gang involvement, which surprised nobody in this city. A brief conversation with the Hotel Bravo's concierge gave him the name of a street with bars where the journalist fraternity shaped their stories and swapped gossip. A good place to start.

The first bar held a handful of patrons. The lack of buzz told Duval this was unlikely to help him. The second wasn't much better. The next one was busy. Most of the tables were occupied and a few men chatted at the bar counter. Better. At the end of the counter a free seat beckoned, adjacent to a squat, middle-aged customer deep in conversation with his companion, his junior by some years. The younger man listened with a frown on his face. Duval ordered a cola. The news programme on the screen above the bartender's head was audible, and most of the men at the counter peered at the set and talked among themselves. The prime item covered the airport attack.

"Broad daylight shooting, eh? Takes some nerve," Duval said to the server, loud enough to be picked up by his chatting neighbours. The nearest man turned to see who was speaking.

"Evening, gentlemen." He nodded to the drinkers. "I came in at the airport today, didn't catch any of that," he said.

"Yeah. It all happened in minutes. Some gringos pissed off the local boys," said the older man, tipping his glass toward the barman.

"Buy you a drink, guys?" asked Duval.

"Never say no, thanks. You been in here before?"

"No. First time in this neck of the woods. I'm only here for a few days, insurance work. Yourselves?"

"I'm Sanchez. Pedro here and me, we work for the newspaper down the street. We cover everything from the baseball season, to politics, to the crime beat. And there's plenty of that to keep us going, Señor. Pedro's my brother's son. I'm teaching him the ropes."

The nephew nodded and smiled at Duval.

"Good to meet you both. I suppose the police will never find out who did this stuff, eh?"

"Word is on the street already, my friend. Nothing stays quiet in this city for long. Manuel Estrada's getting the credit for it."

Sanchez smiled and tapped his glass against Duval's.

"Salud."

"Credit? Surely whoever did it wants to be invisible?"

"Señor, this is El Paso-Juarez. The cartels run this city. Money talks louder than the law. Most of the time, money *is* the law. Word is Estrada's holding a huge garden party tomorrow for his wife's birthday. You can bet all the top local officials, including the cops, are invited. And they'll be there."

"Are the press invited, too?"

"Some will be there, Señor. The puppets. I'm not on that exalted list," said Sanchez, downing his drink in one shot.

"Another round please, barman," said Duval, pushing his glass across the counter. The journalists didn't resist the offered drinks.

Two hours later, the pressmen were ready to go home to sleep off the effects of the flow of free drinks. In the meantime, their new friend had casually milked them of all the information he needed.

According to Sanchez, the hacienda for the birthday party the next day was near the edge of the city, halfway on the route toward the airport.

Duval recalled it well from his drive from the airport to the hotel. A small, wooded hill overlooked the sprawling gardens. The party would kick off with a typical, massive lunch. Musicians and liquor would be in steady supply with revels in full swing by mid-evening and continue well into the following morning.

The journalists lumbered into a taxi outside the bar and disappeared into the darkened night. Duval walked for a few streets and found what he was looking for. In the poorer quarters of the city, pawnshops proliferated; open all hours of the day and night. These shops paid no heed to registration laws for the sale and purchase of weapons. The range of high-powered rifles available would not have been out of place in an armoury.

The owner of the outlet smelled of alcohol and cheap tobacco. He asked no questions of Duval as a bunch of dollars changed hands. The marksman left the pawnshop with his weapon and ammunition, wrapped in an anonymous cardboard box. A good night's work. One more piece of business remained, which he'd look after early next day.

Scheduled daily departure flights from El Paso included a connection to Los Angeles, leaving soon after ten in the evening. After breakfast, Duval confirmed his seat for the flight. Check-in time allowed was forty-five minutes. With only hand luggage that would pose no problem.

He rented a grey, nondescript Ford from the local car hire, paying for three days. His reconnaissance of the area around the hacienda didn't take long. The hillside gave unobstructed views across the surrounding gardens. From no more than a hundred and fifty metres, everything happening at the birthday party would be clear. Trees near the crest of the bank provided enough cover. This would do. He drove a short distance away to find a secluded area to test the rifle sight's calibration. A few shots at a target a couple of hundred metres away told him he needed only a marginal adjustment.

Duval returned to Hotel Bravo around three o'clock. His knee hurt. Damn, he had forgotten to bring his medicines with him. The pharmacy along the street provided painkillers and he settled down to rest for the afternoon. The television showed again the aftermath at the scene of the airport shooting, blatantly followed by the news of Estrada's party later in the day. No-one had claimed responsibility for the murders. The head of the local police force told the cameras investigations were underway, but currently had no clues pointing toward the perpetrators. He was a prime guest at the birthday function.

The trestle tables stretched in several rows around the huge garden. A professional kitchen team hired to supply his guests with adequate food and drink worked hard to please Estrada. They had catered here for previous parties. The Mexican's reputation as a generous tipper for looking after his family and friends was incentive to provide the best possible service. The downside incentive was not so pleasant.

Cars began to arrive around midday, valet-parked outside the hacienda by half a dozen of his own people. Armed security with weapons visible surprised no-one. Many of the invited assembly brought their own personal bodyguards. This was El Paso-Juarez.

A platform offered ample room for the band, one of the best local combos. In front of the stage, the dancing surface covered several dozen square metres. Estrada's wife loved flowers and large clusters of flora decked the tables and walls of the buildings within the compound. Waiters greeted guests on arrival with trays of champagne and whatever other drinks they preferred. Today marked a special, family day each year, where the drugs boss showed the world what a loving, caring husband and father he was. Lunch started a couple of hours after noon and would run on for hours. As mine host, Estrada made constant visits to each table, being photographed with his friends and their families. This was as much business as pleasure in this city's web of connections. The noise grew louder as the day progressed. Many of the guests were already drunk. Laughter and music filled the garden. Children squealed, playing around their parents. The heat of the sun receded in the late afternoon. By seven-thirty, the musicians introduced dance music to the repertoire, but nobody approached the dance floor. Except Manuel Estrada. Everyone knew the annual routine.

He stepped onto the stage and took a microphone from the band, which had stopped playing.

"My dear amigos. I want to extend my thanks to all of you for coming to the birthday celebrations of my beloved wife, Isabella. Our family is your family, my house is your house, my home is your home. My dear Isabella graces my life and has given me our five beautiful children. She is the one who holds our family in her wonderful hands, and we hold her in our hearts. I am a blessed man. Come here, my dear."

Isabella smiled and joined her husband on the platform. A waiter offered a tray with two glasses of champagne.

"I give you a toast to the most lovely woman and the best wife in the world. My dear Isabella."

The crowd roared back, "To Isabella."

Loud applause followed, while several of the other ladies in the garden smiled inwardly, remembering when Manuel Estrada was alone with each of them, dear Isabella was furthest from his thoughts.

With a kiss for his wife and an expansive wave of his arms, he called to the bandleader, "Maestro, music for dancing, if you please."

In moments, the floor filled. The second part of the day had begun.

The dusk segued into darkness around the hacienda, contrasting the bright lights in the garden. Duval picked his spot between two bushes and prepared the rifle sights. There would only be time for one shot. He panned the weapon across the festivities, pleased with the focus on his purchase. The music was in full swing, and the dancing area packed with men, women, and children. The large frame of Manuel Estrada careened in and out of a mass of revellers as he linked arms with several men and women with gusto in a lively conga. With too much movement for a clean shot, the hitman waited. Finally, his target mopped his brow and walked toward a table at the edge of the dance floor. He sat down beside a pretty girl in her teens and kissed her gently on the forehead. She smiled and offered a half-full glass to Estrada. Duval squeezed the trigger and watched for the Mexican to fall. A split second before he fired, the glass slipped from his prey's hand. Manuel Estrada leaned forward to see where the glass had fallen. That split-second spared his life, but not that of his eldest daughter who had given the glass to her father moments before. The bullet intended for her father pierced the neck of the girl, killing her instantly.

"Damn," muttered Duval. The noise of the band covered the rifle shot from that distance, and continued until replaced with screaming as people saw the blood pumping onto the daughter's party dress. A second shot was out of the question. In seconds, the gunman retraced his steps to the Ford and drove away toward the airport. Traffic was light. Not enough time had passed to expect any police sirens. Duval stopped in a lay-by after five minutes and threw the cloth-wrapped weapon far into the woods by the roadside. Ten minutes later, he presented his flight ticket in exchange for a boarding pass and moved to the departure gate.

Back at the hacienda, a half-drunk Chief of Police attempted to bring some order into the mayhem. His thought processes weren't sharp enough to order an immediate check on outgoing flights. When the squad cars arrived at the airport an hour later, Rikko Duval was five miles above the ground on his way to Los Angeles.

# CHAPTER 32

The media had a field day, both locally and internationally. Closer to home, journalists were guarded in reports linking the deaths of Cy Foster and his colleagues with the murder of Manuel Estrada's eldest daughter. Internationally, no such inhibitions cramped the stories. Rumours of DEA revenge for the killing of three of their own mingled with accounts leaked by rival gangs claiming credit for the hit. Three days after the shooting, the funeral attracted hundreds of mourners. Estrada's grief hadn't dulled his brain. He heard the opinions of who was responsible. He discounted all of them. Much as the DEA was at war with all the cartels, it didn't include assassinations like these. Takedowns, yes, but not measured targeting as this had been, with so many dignitaries present, including high-ranking, law enforcement personnel. For all the baying from his competition, he sensed in his gut they didn't have the *cojones* for such an outrageous act. That left international competition. Ahmed Fadi. He'd make that snivelling bastard suffer for this.

In Istanbul, the object of his growing desire for revenge philosophically accepted the accidental killing of Estrada's daughter as a blip. Collateral damage.

"There'll be other opportunities to take him out," he told Duval on the international line.

"Don't underestimate him," said the assassin. "I agree he's a bit crazy, but he's not stupid. He's not likely to react immediately. He'll think this through, and I've no doubt he'll figure you're responsible. I'm not the only person for hire in this market. Apart from sending his own people after you, he could engage professionals. It's time to be careful until we get another shot at him."

"Sound advice, my friend. Let me think about it and I'll be in touch again soon."

Rikko Duval heard the line go dead. The missed hit in El Paso-Juarez was just one of those bad days at the office. A lifetime of being careful dictated most actions have counter-actions. He had to make some arrangements. He dialled another number and a polished voice sounded on the other end.

"Good afternoon. This is the general manager, Reliance Bank in Gibraltar. How may I help you?"

"This is Robert Cavendish. I'd like to take some of your time tomorrow afternoon around three to review my portfolio with you and to make some money transfers. Will you be free?"

"Of course, Mister Cavendish. It'll be my pleasure. See you tomorrow," he said, reaching for the embossed business card with the Interpol chief's number.

Marcel Benoit thanked the bank manager for the information and issued instructions for his agents to fly to Gibraltar on the midday flight next day to stake out the bank.

# CHAPTER 33

Heavy bandaging still covered her eye, but May-Ling had improved steadily over the previous few days. Her official status remained serious, but the critical alert had lessened. Speech had returned but Doctor Spencer warned Jack not to tire his wife too much. He was allowed to be with her for half an hour twice a day while awake.

"What are going to do about Duval?" she asked.

He pressed her hand softly and replied, "Don't you worry yourself about Duval, sweetheart. We'll take care of him soon enough."

"What are you not telling me? I know when you're holding stuff back from me."

Jack looked away from her.

*How to open the issue with her?*

She beat him to it.

"You're thinking about the baby, right?"

He stammered, "You didn't tell me you were expecting."

"You silly man. I thought I might be pregnant but only got confirmation the day Jules and I went to King's Cross. The doctor tells me it's unharmed."

"Yes. He told me when I first met him. I'm worried to hell about you getting well. And there's other news I suppose you should know."

"Tell me."

"Cy Foster was murdered in El Paso when he flew back from Jules' funeral."

"Oh, Jack, that's horrible. Was it Duval?"

"No. Marcel thinks Manuel Estrada's people did it. But we think Duval's been in El Paso in the past few days. Somebody assassinated Estrada's daughter in his front garden during his wife's birthday celebrations. We've been told the DEA people weren't involved and rival gang hits don't go down that way."

"Then who?"

"On the night you and Jules went to the station, we took out the shipment from Mexico intended for Ahmed Fadi, just as Jules had planned. To create a rift between the two of them."

May-Ling was quiet. Jack said nothing. She spoke again.

"So Fadi thinks Estrada's double-crossed him and sends Duval to deliver a message by killing his daughter?"

"No. Killing his daughter would serve no purpose. We think he meant to shoot Manuel Estrada himself. The bullet hit the wrong target."

"My God, Jack. You really think so? What happens next?"

"No way of telling for sure, but it won't finish there. The DEA guys are tracking Estrada's movements. Marcel is trying to get a line on Fadi. They've all promised to keep us in the loop."

His wife stared at him. "Then you and Malky'll make sure they finish their personal business, right?"

Jack nodded. "Jules always said you thought clearer than any of us, even if you're injured. Yes, if they don't take each other out, we intend to lend them a hand. Anyway, you have to get some rest. I'll be back tomorrow, sweetheart."

He leaned forward and kissed her forehead. May-Ling closed her eyes. Her thoughts slipping into sleep included Jules Townsend, Cy Foster, Manuel Estrada, Ahmed Fadi, her beloved Jack and an unborn baby. Even in a half-sleep state she realised something had changed in her husband, something ruthless she had never seen before.

# CHAPTER 34

The early flight from Casablanca landed in Gibraltar in time for Rikko Duval to be at the bank office minutes after opening time.

"Mister Cavendish, I wasn't expecting you until this afternoon," said the general manager as his secretary led his visitor into the private office.

"My apologies. Last minute change of travel schedules," said Duval. "Can you still assist me at such short notice?"

"Of course, of course. Please, have a seat. Coffee with no sugar as usual?"

The officer buzzed his intercom and gave the order to his assistant. In a few minutes, she appeared with a silver tray with the coffee and assorted biscuits.

"Please ensure we aren't disturbed," he said, pressing a desk switch to illuminate the privacy sign outside of the room. The secretary retreated and closed the door behind her. Instructions were absolute never to interrupt the manager when the light switched to the 'occupied' setting.

Duval picked up immediately on the manager's nervousness. Small beads of sweat showed on his brow, even in the air-conditioned office. He touched his tie and smoothed his jacket repeatedly. He had never seen him in anything but sophisticated banker mode. Something was wrong. His decision to switch his timing to this earlier arrival was a normal ruse he used to stay a step ahead of any circumstance. Keep everyone else off guard. Part of his SAS training included doing the unexpected.

"What did you have in mind today, Mister Cavendish? You said you wanted to make some money transfers?"

His client removed a folded paper from his jacket and handed it across the desk.

"Yes. I need to make these two transactions now. The last time I moved funds we did it together from your computer. For confidentiality, can we do the same now?"

The manager's hand trembled a little as he took the paper and read the instructions.

"But…but this is almost all of your deposits with Reliance Bank, Mister Cavendish."

"Some temporary alternative investments. Don't worry, I'll be moving the money back to your bank after a short while."

The pair of transactions amounted to almost thirty million dollars. The first recipient bank was in the Cayman Islands, the second in the Dominican Republic.

"I… I…"

"Do we have a problem with these? We've done large sums before."

"No, no. There's no problem."

If the man had been nervous before, he was close to panic now.

After a moment or two, he regained his composure. He remembered Benoit had told him to act normally if Cavendish turned up at the bank. Normal included doing standard business such as money transfers for his client. And he had made the telephone call as directed.

He recovered his nerve and said, "Mister Cavendish, forgive me, it's just that we seldom lose such a large amount of our valued customer deposits, even temporarily. Of course, I'll do these with you right now."

The computer on the desk lit up. The manager keyed in his own password, then invited Duval to counter-key with his own personal code. Seated at the screen with his customer standing behind watching as the instructions fed into the system, the bank officer didn't catch Duval's eyes scanning the desktop. The Interpol business card of Marcel Benoit was unmistakable, leaning upright against the telephone console. Duval's instincts had proved correct, yet again. Now he understood the nervousness.

Somehow the bastards had tracked the payments to here. His forward planning was about to save him thirty million dollars.

"How are we doing? These should be in the other banks' systems in minutes, shouldn't they?"

"Yes, they're irreversibly in the system now. See, here are the reference numbers for you," the general manager said, handing over a sheet with the printed codes.

"I'm grateful for your help," said Duval.

Without warning, his right hand jabbed forward in a karate punch, catching the manager in the throat. The man jerked backward in his chair. In seconds his head was in a deadlock. A sharp twist snapped his neck. Duval eased the body on to the carpet and sat down at the computer. In a matter of minutes, he dispatched instructions to the two earlier receiving banks with coded details for forwarding the received monies into several account names with other banks. These banks resided in jurisdictions less accessible to the prying eyes of international authorities.

He moved across the floor to let himself out and called back as he went.

"Thank you for all your help. I'll be in touch soon," a farewell meant only for the secretary's ears as he closed the door.

The privacy light remained on and stayed that way until two hours later.

* * *

The Interpol agents showed their badges to the secretary who reluctantly let them open her chief's door. Minutes later, her screams and hysterics echoed through the bank. She herself would need the ambulance that would be of no use to her boss. The agents relayed the news to Marcel Benoit in Lyons before calling in local police and detectives to cordon off the murder scene.

"Clever bastard," said Marcel to the agent who called. "Jules said he was intelligent. He's a thinker alright. Okay, I want you both to stay put and work with the local head of police. Use my name, he's a friend. The likeliest exit is by plane and I'm sure he's no longer in Gibraltar. Get a hold of the CCTV scans at the airport. He walks with a limp, and it might show up. If he does, try to find which departure gate he used. That'll give us a flight and a destination."

Within hours, the fast response through the assistance of the local police chief gave them the destination of the killer. The limp clearly noticeable on the CCTV coverage made identification simple. After leaving the check-in counter, Duval made an unhurried walk through the forecourt of the departure hall and turned left. With no hand luggage visible, Marcel Benoit assumed the flight would be taking his quarry home. The flight had already been called as the former soldier walked down the covered archway to his plane. The destination Casablanca, a city easy to remain hidden in, but at least the hunters now had a target area to zone in on. So far, the mobile phone and email trails had given no clues. The man was astute. He would know not to have the SIM card live until he needed to use the phone if it was even still in his possession. Apart from routine detective work, the best chance remained with the technical experts by cyber-tracking whatever computer device Duval used, either a laptop or a computer at some internet café.

* * *

Rikko Duval's life and freedom depended on anonymity and invisibility. His routine was non-routine. Blending in with the background had become second nature to him. He wore neutral-coloured clothing. Transport in Casablanca was always by foot or by taxi, no car ownership registration, even in a false name. Vehicles are too easily tracked. He stopped taxis streets away from where he lived and walked the rest of the way home. No shops in the area around his dwelling enjoyed his regular patronage. When he did make purchases, these were in cash, no credit card receipts or records anywhere. His nondescript villa blended in with several identical buildings set back from the main street in a lower middle-class district. Laundry and cleaning of his residence he took care of himself, with no maid or maintenance workers.

The late morning flight from Gibraltar had been on schedule. He closed the villa's front door and checked the rooms in rote, a security habit as natural to him as breathing. He kicked off his shoes, poured some sparkling water and sat down to think. The close call at the bank disturbed him. Until now, his identity had never been an issue.

*Where had it leaked? Fadi? Somebody in Fadi's camp?*

He'd need to talk to Fadi today. The Interpol card on the bank manager's desk meant they had been at the bank before. No records existed at the bank to lead them here to Casablanca. But was he safe in Morocco? How much did they know? The obvious link tied in Jules and his fucking interfering bastards. Well, Townsend had bought his. With any luck the Chinese bitch wouldn't make it either. Her Scots husband and his Irish mate posed a different proposition. Their reputations in the special services community were well-founded. They were dangerous operators and if still involved in this, the whole ball game had just elevated to a new and riskier level. He'd have to do something about them. But just what? This would take some time to think through. His knee hurt like hell, a sign of stress. He reached for the medication and switched on the television news, the only channel he ever watched.

The newscasts ran in English, French and Arabic in Morocco. He was fluent in French and understood some basic Arabic. The picture flashing across the screen jolted him. His own face, ten years younger, looked back at him.

*Fuck. How the hell?*

"Police authorities are seeking to interview this man in connection with a murder at Reliance Bank in Gibraltar earlier today. It's believed he may be in the Casablanca area. If you know this man, or have seen him at any time, please contact the number shown below. Do not approach him," said the announcer. "We repeat, do not approach him. He is dangerous and may kill again."

No mention of his limp. They'd missed out on that. He moved quickly. Duval always had back-up plans for a rapid exit wherever he located. The early evening darkness helped.

The cloth rucksack's sewn-in pockets held four passports in different identities as well as seven thousand dollars in hundred bills. A grey thobe covered his denims and sweatshirt. The traditional Arabic male clothing provided easy camouflage. A red and white checked, cotton scarf hid his head and part of his face.

He retrieved the mobile telephone from the bedside table drawer and inserted the SIM card. There was only one number on speed dial. Ahmed Fadi answered within two rings.

"You have a major leak. The police know about the payments to Reliance Bank," he said without introduction. "It means they've tapped into you on the other business. I'm on my way to Algeria. Meet me at the Livic Hotel, near the docks. Mid-morning, day after tomorrow. I've got some ideas for you. I understand you're a careful man but be extra cautious."

"My friend, I can't move on a whim like this."

"It's not a whim. Interpol's involved. Probably Jack Calder and his mate, too. You still have the Mexican issue to deal with. Be there."

The drug boss wasn't used to taking orders, but Duval had delivered flawlessly every time he'd been asked, apart from the blip with Estrada's daughter. His gut told him his hitman was right.

"Okay. The day after tomorrow. See you there," said Fadi.

Duval put the mobile back in the drawer.

In a side street a couple of hundred metres from the villa, a dark-blue Nissan's windscreen had a slight layer of dust, indicating the vehicle had been parked for at least a day or two, the ignition key still in place. Car theft is not common in Arabic countries. The door handle turned in his hand. He slid into the driving seat and shoved his rucksack across to the passenger side. The gas tank showed almost full, no need to stop for a refill. He eased away and headed out eastward toward the Algerian border. At a steady speed he would reach the crossing point in ten hours, faster if traffic was light.

The border control officer accepted his passport and opened the first page. Two hundred-dollar notes transferred from the document to the officer's pocket. He handed the passport back with a wave and a *"Maa'ah salama"*. Duval entered the country and headed for Bechar airport, a forty-kilometre drive from the border crossing.

The airport was a feeder to Algiers for the main international routes. Air Algerie scheduled regular flights to the capital. He nudged the Nissan into a space at the side of the long-term car park, close to the entrance to the terminal. His practiced eye registered nothing out of the ordinary in the way of potential watchers. No casual, standby personnel, and no sign of occupied vehicles within sight of the entrance. He tossed the thobe and onto the back seat and reached for the rucksack. The French passport and a few more dollars slipped into his pocket. A small cloth wiped down the driving wheel and the door handle, leaving no trace of fingerprints. By the time this vehicle was recovered, Duval would be long gone. The next flight to Algiers departed in fifty minutes. A one-way ticket paid in cash secured a seat in economy class.

# CHAPTER 35

After leaving the Balkans and his Serbian name of Viktor Bodan behind him, Ahmed Fadi's nous and determination over several years had built up a powerful network out of Turkey, supplying drugs from Afghanistan into the European cities. An intelligent strategist, he valued planning. Planning also meant taking care in everything he touched. This latest unfolding threat from Interpol caused him little concern so long as he remained in Istanbul. The network of bribed officials provided a comfort level few could afford. Outside of the country was a different matter.

The phone call from Duval disturbed him. The tracking of his money flow demanded a complete change of routine.

*Just how much did the authorities know?*

The information available from banks wasn't something he could stop. Money transfers are recorded, and large amounts stand out quickly. He had to overhaul the system with his accountants. Most of his men were survivors from the days in the Balkans, but he'd arrange a personal back check on each of them, just in case.

*You can never be too careful.*

The proposed meeting in Algiers made sense. He had contacts in the city, useful middlemen who channelled much of the drug shipments on to Europe, but commercial air transport was out of the question. He called in his aide-de-camp. A trusted, solid, right-hand man, he had been with Fadi for more than thirty years.

"Yes, boss?" the voice came from the depths of the man's boots. "What's up?"

"We may have a leak in the organisation, maybe not," said Fadi. "I want you to run a check on everybody who handles our payments. Interpol's on to the money we sent to Gibraltar. I want to know if our other payment streams are affected. Put a hold on any bank accounts currently in the system for anything other than ordinary commercial needs. Transfer any major balances to a safe account. The accountants can do that. Tell them I need a report on the cash position as soon as possible."

"I can tell you it's tight, Ahmed. The money we expected from London's dried up."

"Send a message down the line to the distributors. No more credit terms for the meantime. Cash or no merchandise. The dealers won't like it, but if you have to squeeze a few balls, do so."

The aide nodded and turned to leave.

"Something else," said Fadi. "We're going to Algiers for a meeting the day after tomorrow. Talk to the plane charter guys. Use one of the smaller company names. You and two of our men will come with me. Contact our people at both airports. I want us moving in and out without having to show our passports. Understand?"

"Yes."

"And get them to check out the Livic Hotel, near the dockside."

* * *

"We think we have a lead on where he lives, Marcel."

The head of the detective force in Casablanca had responded to his old friend's request to put a red alert on the hunt for the Gibraltar killer.

"My men have criss-crossed the city, showing his picture to anybody and everybody. We got lucky. A newspaper seller thinks this guy lives in a villa along from his corner stall. You said not to intercept at this stage. What do you want us to do now?"

"Good work, mon ami. If your men can keep a watch on the location, I'll fly across as soon as possible. Frankly, between you and me, there's a lot more at stake here than the murder of the bank manager. Also, the place may be rigged with explosives. The man's a genius with that stuff. Please tread carefully."

"Understood. I'll meet you at the airport. Call me when you expect to arrive. Au revoir."

This must be a big affair when the Interpol boss himself flies in to take charge, the head of detectives thought.


Five hours after the call, Marcel shook hands with his friend, and they drove to the villa.

"I have five men surrounding the place, but no movement and no lights have shown anywhere. No-one has gone in or come out."

"He may not be in there, but as I said, we have to be cautious. You have someone here from the explosives squad, I presume?"

"Of course. Shall we?"

Marcel led the way. The pair approached the villa and peered through the windows. Through the light curtains they could see nobody inside. The head of detectives motioned for his bomb expert to come forward to check the door. In minutes he indicated no booby trap on the front door. To everyone's surprise, when he tried the handle, the door opened. An unlocked entrance, either a decoy or showing nothing to hide inside.

The place was unoccupied. Marcel ordered everyone to wear rubber gloves and to walk with care. Within half an hour, all the rooms had been thoroughly checked. Nothing out of the ordinary. The bedroom wardrobe held male clothing, mostly black and bland colours. The kitchen was tidy, no cups or glasses to remove to test for possible DNA samples. No sign of a computer or laptop. If this was Duval's villa, the lack of computers would fit in with the assumption he always used external sites for messaging.

"We found these in the bedside table drawer, sir," said one of the officers, holding a mobile telephone and an opened box of strong painkillers. He handed them to his boss, who gave the phone to Marcel.

"Hmm. Let's see what it tells us." The on-switch lit the screen, the SIM card still inside. The last call showed an overseas number dated the previous day. Marcel recognised the code for Turkey. He noted the number and asked the officer to put the phone and the tablets back as he found them. "It's not definite, but I'm almost certain this is our man's place. He may return here, and he may not, *mon ami*, but no point in leaving a calling card, eh? Okay, we've done enough for now. He's disappeared for the moment. God only knows where he'll show up next."

* * *

Where Duval showed up next was familiar terrain. Algeria had been a regular stopping-off city for assignments over the years. Police surveillance in the country was notoriously lax. A man of Duval's calling was unlikely to attract the attention of the authorities. The Livic Hotel, a low-quality establishment, fitted his taste well. Nobody asked questions, cash the usual mode of payment, an ideal place to go quietly about his business. He locked the room door and slid the chain across for extra measure. The pressure pain on his knee from the long drive nagged at him. He lay down on the bed after swallowing a couple of painkillers. The idea he had to discuss with Fadi was clear in his head; he needed the Serbian to buy in. Midnight had long passed before he lapsed into sleep.

# CHAPTER 36

With the bandages removed, the effect of the blast on the left side of May-Ling's face revealed damage to her ear as well as the eye. The nurses had shaved her head to give clean access to the wounds. Her normally healthy skin had a pallor Jack hadn't seen before. His wife was still very sick. Doctor Spencer spoke to them together at May-Ling's request.

"My husband has to know everything you tell me," she had insisted. Jack sat at the opposite side of the bed from the doctor. His clipboard held several sheets of paper, the detailed medical test reports.

"Mrs Calder, I'm pleased to say you're past the initial dangerous phase. Often in the first two or three days, delayed effects can arise from the blast injuries, particularly to the head. The brain is a highly sensitive organ," he said. "As I told you before, much of the force of the explosion was shielded by your companions when the bomb went off. Nonetheless, you did suffer severe trauma. The x-rays show us a small hairline fracture at the base of the skull at the back of your head. Healing from that should be quick. The news on your left eye is less encouraging. I'm afraid you may lose up to fifty percent of the vision. The cornea has been distorted and dislocated which is difficult to repair. We can make a final call on that in a few weeks."

Jack gripped his wife's hand gently and she squeezed back.

"What else, Doctor," he said.

"The left eardrum was perforated, which will cause some diminution in hearing, but not deafness. The effects on the shoulder and the left side of the body will leave mild scarring, but no permanent damage."

"What about the baby?" said May-Ling.

"Your own physical well-being speaks volumes, Mrs Calder. So far, everything's in good shape."

A faint smile appeared on her face, and she squeezed Jack's hand again. He sensed he was a stranger looking in on this scenario. The fatherhood warmth he should be feeling was absent. Of course, he loved his wife. More now than ever before. The nights he spent alone at home waiting to come to the hospital each morning offered scant sleep. The nightmares hadn't revisited him, as he half expected they might. Instead, his mind kept coming back to Rikko Duval. Back to Jules Townsend. Dead, Jules Townsend. Dead. Killed by Rikko Duval. The mantra rattled around his head. He realised Doctor Spencer was talking to him.

"We should leave her to rest now, Mister Calder. A word outside if I may?" he said.

"Of course, Doctor." He leaned over and kissed his wife on the forehead. "I'll be back later tonight, sweetheart. I love you."

The doctor walked Jack along the corridor away from the detectives sitting guard outside May-Ling's room.

"Mister Calder, I'm aware of your deep concern for your wife. I can tell you she is out of danger now but will need some months of rehabilitation with her eye and the ear damage. She'll be relatively okay after all of this."

"I'm grateful."

The medical man held up his hand, cutting Jack off. "Right now, I'm also worried about you, Mister Calder."

"Me?"

"Yes, you. As a doctor, I can't miss the way you react in the room when you're with your wife. I understand your past history, and possibly some of your present activity overlaps with that. You show classic signs of a man about to explode, Mister Calder. Anger is a powerful emotion, and a destructive one, often destroying the person trying to grapple with it. I've no doubt you're a strong individual physically, with more courage than the average person could ever hope to have. The danger lies in your mental state. I can recommend another colleague of mine who may be able to help you."

"I appreciate your concern," said Jack. "But I don't need anybody to tell me how to cope with my mind."

"I think..."

"Perhaps you think too much. Perhaps you should concentrate on getting my wife well," Jack snapped. "I'll look after myself, thanks."

He turned abruptly and strode back down the corridor, past the guards without a word to any of them.

"Something wrong, Doc?" one of them asked.

Doctor Spencer shook his head.

"No, nothing wrong. The man's got a lot on his mind, that's all."

Inside he had a different opinion.


Jack switched on the television and poured himself a Scotch. The tightness at the back of his shoulders nagged at him. He stretched his elbows back a few times, trying to relax the muscles. The sound from the news programme was only a noise and he turned the set off. Another Scotch with a splash of water went down easily. Doctor Spencer's words revolved around his head.

*Worried about me? My mental state? What the fuck?*

The third glass of Scotch sat untouched. The series of events from leaving London to take down the Turkish shipment, the explosions at the train station, Jules' funeral, Cy's murder, all the way to the conversation tonight in the hospital, ran like an unavoidable tape. He felt his body seize, his fists clenching, then easing down.

*The man was right. Damn.*

He called the hospital and asked for Doctor Spencer.

"Hold the line please, I'll page him for you," said the ward duty-nurse. Moments later he came online.

"Hello, Doc. This is Jack Calder. I'm sorry I behaved like a dickhead earlier. A lot of stuff's going on in my head right now with the attack on my wife and Jules being killed. I had no right to speak to you the way I did. I really want to apologise."

"No need for apologies, Mister Calder. I've seen what this is doing to you, and just wanted to suggest a way to deal with it. The fact you're calling now tells me you're starting to become aware of the potential effects when our family and friends are attacked or threatened."

"I hear you, Doc, but hey, I've seen friends killed in action. I've watched kids and old people slaughtered in places you'd never want to imagine."

"I understand. However, none of these matches coping with death and life-threatening injuries to the people we love, Mister Calder."

"Okay. Well, I just wanted to say sorry."

"My offer is open at all times, if you want to talk to me or one of my colleagues."

"Thanks again. See you tomorrow, Doc."

Jack put down the phone and caught his breath for a moment. Like a child he began to weep. The tension flowed out through his sobbing. He had cried like this only once before in his life. After the murder of a former buddy, when he realised how much the pointlessness of his death related to the suicide of his father all those years ago when Jack was just a child.

He drank the third Scotch and poured another. A mid-morning meeting at ISP was scheduled for next day but seemed a long way away.

Donnie Mullen led the discussion but didn't sit at the top of the table. Jules' place. Paul Manning and Malky already had coffee mugs in front of them when Jack entered the boardroom. Nobody commented on his arrival, ten minutes late. The hangover dressed his face. Malky poured another mug, straight black, and handed it to his buddy, with a squeeze of his shoulder.

"Morning, Jack," said Donnie.

This was the first formal get-together since the King's Cross tragedy.

"Let's get started. First order of priority concerns operations. We've reinforced the red alert in all our branches. So far, nothing else out of the ordinary to report."

Jack cleared his throat. "What are we going to do about Duval? And Fadi? And Estrada? We still have a clean-up contract from Chuck Morrow's insurance group. Are we forgetting our fucking priorities?"

"Whoa, Jack. We're all on the same side here. We feel the same as you about what these bastards did to May-Ling and Jules. And Cy. But we can't go chasing shadows. Paul talked to Alan Rennie last night. He's got some news for us. Paul?"

"Interpol nailed down where Duval's been living. A villa in Casablanca. Marcel went himself. Our man wasn't at home and unlikely to be back again. He knows his cash payments were tracked to Gibraltar. By the way, he topped a bank manager in his office and walked out as calm as you please," said Paul. "Not only that, they checked his account. He transferred most of his money out of the bank while he was taking the guy out. Untraceable now. This is one cool criminal."

"So, no trace of him?' asked Malky, topping up the coffees.

"A little chink of light," said Paul, holding out his mug. "They found a mobile phone with a recent call to Turkey. Duval won't use the device again, but the number he called is traceable. They presumed Fadi was on the other end and Interpol put a tracker on it. Fadi didn't remove the SIM card, making his phone location traceable. Marcel's people already know he's left Istanbul and landed in Algiers last night."

"Then what's keeping us?" said Jack. "Let's get to Algiers now and nail the bastards."

"Not so fast, Jack. It's not as simple as you think," said Donnie. "Marcel's men are on the ground trying to pinpoint where Fadi is. Chances are he's meeting Duval. Algiers isn't an easy place to hunt down bad guys. I think we should wait for a further heads up from Marcel. Paul, you'll keep fielding info from him and Alan."

"Donnie's right, Jack," said Malky. "We should wait our chance and make sure we get them good when we take them down. That goes for yer Mexican pal, too."

Jack shrugged, practicality overriding his urge for action.

"C'mon, mate, let's go see yer wife," said Malky. "I'll drive."

# CHAPTER 37

A previous, awkward, cross-forces incident involving the mistaken-identity shooting of a local detective by Interpol agents some years earlier in Algiers made it politically appropriate for Marcel Benoit to decide to enlist the help of the local force. He didn't mention Fadi by name, only a request to monitor a possible, international criminal operator. The triangulation on Fadi's phone zoned in on the dockside area. Two of the Interpol men joined four Algerian detectives as they waited final directions on where the signals led.

The Turkish contingent left their hostel and walked the hundred metres to the Livic Hotel. Duval had booked a private room on the ground floor. He arrived in time to greet his paymaster. Fadi ordered his men to sit outside on guard while he and Duval transacted their business.

"This is bad news about Interpol. How can you be so sure?" said Fadi.

"The manager was shitting himself from the minute I walked in, and Marcel Benoit's card was on his table."

"Who's he?"

"The head of Interpol. I'm surprised you don't know him."

"I don't socialise in these circles."

Duval grinned. "Quite so."

"What did the manager say when you left him."

"Nothing. He was dead."

Fadi smiled.

"The police would have used their own resources to trace your money payments, but you have to wonder where they got your name in the first place," said Duval.

"I'm checking on everybody in the chain. Believe me, I'm always very careful, but you're right about the second thing. I've no idea why they should be tracking me unless the Mexican's slipped his mouth somewhere."

"No. He wouldn't do that on purpose. It comes back to Townsend's people. They were the ones who hit your warehouse, for sure. The black guy's dead, by the way."

"Oh? Where did you get that from?"

"He was the head of the DEA in El Paso. Estrada's guns shot him at the airport the day I landed. I think that might open the door to solve your issues with your Mexican friend and the ISP."

"ISP have no fight with me," said Fadi.

"I think you're wrong. Jules Townsend probably figured out you're behind the New Bond Street stuff. Where the guy in El Peso came into the picture, I can't say, but it makes logical sense to me if they're part of the same deal."

"How would this solve issues with both?"

"You talk to Manuel. You tell him your information sources say Jack Calder killed his daughter. The black guy ordered the hit as part of the campaign, including the hijacking of the drugs in Antalya. Propose to carry on your partnership plans from before."

"What else?"

"You combine efforts with him to put ISP out of business permanently."

"Meaning eliminating Mister Calder and the rest of his partners?"

"Yes," said Duval.

For the second time in the meeting, Ahmed Fadi smiled.

"This suits your purpose too, I think," he said. "If I'm not mistaken, you have a score to settle, too?"

"You could say that. I won't be sorry when they're all dead." This time, Rikko Duval didn't smile. He stood up and excused himself.

"I'm going for a pee. I'll be back in a few minutes." Duval left the salon, passed the guards outside and walked to the end of the corridor. Some way down from the corner, the washrooms tucked in at the end of the adjoining corridor. He pushed the door and went in.

The message flashed to the Interpol agent signalling the Livic Hotel as the source of the pings from Fadi's SIM card. The lead local detective took over. The posse moved in giving no chance for the guards to react. The appearance of half a dozen armed men meant no resistance. A belated shout to Fadi served only to alert the detectives to his presence inside the salon. The police officers ushered the guards inside to join their boss. Faced with an array of guns and a police badge, Ahmed Fadi stayed calm.

"What's going on here? This is a private business meeting. You must be mistaking us for someone else," he said to the man with the badge.

"We'll see about that. Meantime you're coming with us."

"Are we under arrest?"

"You're assisting authorities with their enquiries will do for now. Cuff them."

The detectives handcuffed the quartet and led them out of the salon.

Duval returned from the washroom and heard the noise before he reached the corner of the corridor. He realised something was badly wrong. An exit door next to the men's room led out of the hotel. He eased to the corner of the building. A few metres away a couple of large, windowless vans and another car parked between them carried no signs, but were unmistakably police. From the shadows he watched as Fadi and his guards streamed out with half a dozen other men. In minutes, all three vehicles drove out of the car park. Nobody remained who looked like police. Fadi had held his tongue.

*How the hell did they find us? They're on to Ahmed, that's how, dammit. But they didn't wait around. Means they're not on to me. Yet.*

The hallway back into the hotel was deserted. Duval overheard the concierge talking excitedly on the telephone to somebody. He reached his room on the first floor without incident. The packed rucksack sat untouched in the wardrobe. He picked up the bag, retraced his steps to the back exit door and disappeared into the night.

* * *

The official dinner for International Police Federation Charities in Paris had started when Marcel Benoit's mobile phone vibrated. His attendance as a top-table guest at these official events came with the territory. He glanced at the screen and excused himself. An adjoining room gave him the privacy to call his agent in Algiers.

"Good evening, boss. The local guys arrested four men an hour ago. Three armed guards and one guy in a meeting room. They refuse to say anything until their lawyer arrives. We'll have to wait for him, then we can give you an update."

"Excellent. Was Duval one of them? He's the guy with the limp."

"None of these men has a limp. Maybe he wasn't there tonight."

"Why do you think there would be only one guy in a meeting room? Perhaps they moved in too early? I suggest you get back to the hotel and check if Duval's been seen. Damn. Anyway, it sounds as if they've got Fadi. Let them process him and then we can file for transfer to us for further charges."

"Okay, boss. I'll call you again later."

The Interpol chief pocketed his phone and returned in time for the main course. He didn't relish the interminable after-dinner speeches.

An hour and a half later, the mobile phone in his pocket buzzed again. Marcel welcomed the second excuse to step into the private area. His pleasure would be short-lived.

"Hello. What's happening?"

"Boss. We can't believe this. The lawyer turned up. We weren't allowed into the meeting, only the local cops present. All of them were freed on bail. We never even saw them leave. I reckon the lawyer's a big hitter here."

"Big hitter? Big hitter, my arse!" Marcel stormed. "More like a bundle of fucking money changed hands. I knew I shouldn't have asked the local bastards to get involved. There's no chance of getting another bite at them in Algeria. They're probably flying out as we speak."

"Sorry, boss."

"Not your fault. Any luck on Duval at the hotel?"

"I'm afraid you got that right as well. No name of Duval, but a guest with a limp checked in last night. He paid cash. The room's empty now."

"Damn. Okay. I'll talk to the Chief of Police tomorrow. I won't be surprised if he's on the take as well, but you didn't hear me say so."

"Goodnight, boss."

Marcel didn't return to the dinner. He had a sour taste in his stomach.

* * *

The charter plane taxied for a short distance before taking off north-eastward bound for Turkey. Ahmed Fadi's associates in Algiers had summoned the lawyer and told him to do whatever it took to get the drug boss and his men freed. A couple of high-level names worked, as well as a considerable bribe.

The four-hour flight to Istanbul gave Fadi ample thinking time.

*Was Duval's exit to the washroom too convenient? Was it all an elaborate set-up? What would Duval gain from it? No. The look on his face when I said he had a score to settle was real. And the idea of talking to the buffoon Estrada was good. Well, he knows how to contact me. Let's see if he does.*

The day after arriving back at his fortified home in Kilyos, Ahmed Fadi's instinct proved correct. His right-hand man led his guest into the private sitting room. The drug boss greeted the visitor with respect and waved him toward a seat on the sofa next to his own.

"You never cease to surprise me," said Fadi. "How did you know I'd be here?"

"You're not the only one with contacts in strange places," said Rikko Duval. "A phone call confirmed you'd solved the problem. I also think you were expecting me."

Fadi nodded. "Yes."

"You would figure I'd nothing to do with the police shake down. If I hadn't turned up here, you'd think otherwise, and I'd be a target for you for the rest of your life or mine. Correct?"

"I like the way you think," said Fadi.

"That's what keeps us both alive. I'm sure you've been considering my idea about Manuel Estrada?"

"It's a good strategy, if he bites. If not, we're no worse off. When do you suggest we make contact? Should that be through a third party?"

"No. Direct from you. You wait a little while. Otherwise, if he believes you're responsible for his daughter's killing, he'll think you're gloating. A third-party go-between would increase the number of people knowing what's going on. Estrada's a Latino. He'll be big on personal relationships. You make the call. Leave it for a week."

"Where will you be?"

"I'll be somewhere," said Duval, handing Fadi a piece of paper. "When you need to talk, ring this number. I'll use it only once to receive your call. It will be live for two evenings for five minutes at eight o'clock your time, seven and eight days from now. By then you'll know if Estrada buys in. Whether he does or not, we'll have a fall-back strategy to deal with him, and one for the ISP people. Now, if you can ask one of your men to drive me into the city?"

"Of course," said Fadi, shaking hands goodbye with his guest.

Duval left and the drug boss realised it was the first time the man had given him a handshake. He still didn't know his real name.

# CHAPTER 38

The aftermath of Cy Foster's death reached across all the gangs in El Paso-Juarez. The DEA squads would never admit to an added impetus to their activities solely because of their former leader's killing, but every man and woman in the agency grieved for him. Each wanted to be part of the payback. The normal focus on large drug movements expanded as middle-sized and small operators were also hit hard. This compounded as the major players stepped up attacks on each other's territories, an audacity expected after the murder of Estrada's daughter.

Successive hits on rivals fed the testosterone levels as open warfare spiked across the region. Bravado bred bravado. The DEA welcomed the surge as significant numbers of gang murders made their job easier. The agency officers themselves were more trigger-happy while the culling went on. A gradual slowdown in the killings kicked in after ten days. On the walls inside the agency compound the mug shot photographs with the red 'X's and green question marks had tripled. Dead gang members were replaceable over time, but every mob's normal business routines suffered. The imports, the distribution channels, the dealer networks, the cash middlemen, were all disrupted. Disruption meant loss of trade and squeezed cash flows. Estrada ran the biggest operation and was under most financial pressure. The unexpected call from Ahmed Fadi was timely.

"Manuel, I've just learned about your daughter. Terrible news. My condolences. Our recent little incident is as nothing compared to your family's loss," said Fadi.

"My daughter was a princess. She deserved none of this. I'll find whoever did this if it takes the rest of my life. Thank you for your words."

"I heard a whisper, Manuel, the people responsible were associates of the black guy who hit our shipment."

"Yeah, you bet your ass. The drug agency hombres are going nuts out here."

"No, not them. The British outfit. They call themselves International Security Partners. They're the ones who killed my guys and torched our merchandise. Now their pal's dead, I don't think they're gonna stop at this."

Estrada was silent. Fadi filled the void.

"I know we had words, but I was hoping we could put these aside and work together as planned, my friend. The benefits we discussed by working in partnership haven't changed. And I'm sure we can deal with the bastards who killed your daughter."

The Mexican remained silent. Fadi let him process the conversation.

"Let me think about it and get back to you in a day or two," said Estrada.

"Sure. Take your time. We have to do it right. I look forward to your call."

Ahmed Fadi was pleased with the exchanges.

*Good. At least he's not raging at me for now. This'll work out well.*


In El Paso-Juarez, a bemused drug boss pondered. His daughter smiled at him from a silver-framed photograph at the side of his desk. The grief ate at his stomach. Rage simmered in his veins as he thought about Fadi's call. An unsettled murmuring whispered at the back of his mind. A nagging whisper he fully understood. He put it aside and in its place came a reprise of his rise to his current position in El Paso's gangland.


Fifty years before, Emmanuel Calvi Juan de Estrada came gently into the world. A quiet child, the second eldest in the family, his doting parents scraped and sacrificed to raise the boy and his seven siblings in the squalid slums on the edge of El Paso. Education in the sprawling ghetto came from the Christian friars in the San Juan cluster of schools near his home. Attendance depended on the family's need for he and his brothers and sisters to join the hordes of hawkers around the city. Most of their goods cascaded down through several chains of stolen merchandise. The black market let them eke pesos and centavos along with Yankee money wherever they could. Until he was twelve years old, the boy had never worn shoes. The incident that changed his life came a year later, on his mother's birthday.

The streets had a code and a pecking order. Gangs ran the territories where the hawkers plied their trade. Protection money ensured little or no interference so long as the squeeze was paid on time. The young Manuel's day had not gone well. To start with, he had only a few packs of stolen cigarettes to sell, and the meagre takings barely covered the cost of a few flowers for his mother. Every year, his father made sure the children paid homage to his wife on her birthday. This day was no exception.

The flower seller bargained hard. Manuel walked away from the stall with the present and bumped into his protection money collector, a man twice his age. Several of the street hawkers watched, expecting this to end badly.

"Hola, chavo. You have something for me? You know what day it is, eh?"

"Señor, I will pay you tomorrow. Today was not good. I make very little business. Tomorrow I pay you for sure."

"Chavo, you say your day wasn't good, yet you can afford to buy flowers? What lies you are telling me, eh?"

"These are for my mama, Señor. It's her birthday."

"Well, maybe I take the flowers and tomorrow when you pay me the money you can get these back for your mama."

Adrenaline coursed through Manuel Estrada's body as he realised the man was serious. Whatever happened, he could not return home without his mama's birthday gift.

"No, Señor, you will not take these. I told you, tomorrow you will have your money."

"Ah, chavo. Perhaps you don't hear me too well. Maybe I teach you how to listen better."

The man produced a knife and waved it at the boy. At thirteen, Estrada had already learned if a man threatens you, you either run or you kill him. The man in front of him held the only weapon in sight. Time to run. Something screamed inside his head.

*No, Manuel. If you run from this fight, you are as good as dead.*

The enforcer moved forward. Manuel waited until he was almost touching him, then held out the flowers toward the hand holding the knife.

"That's better, chavo," said the man, lowering his attacking arm. At the last second, the boy threw the flowers into his face and seized the knife arm. His father had taught him how to lever an arm to get someone to release whatever they held. The knife dropped to the ground and the young hawker grabbed it before his assailant recovered his balance. In a single movement, Estrada drove the blade into the man's neck and twisted. Blood spurted from the severed jugular vein. The crowd was silent. Nobody moved. The man was dead. The boy bent down to collect the flowers and walked away from the corpse.

Word sped through the community and reached back to Estrada's father the same evening.

"Manuel. I'm proud of you. You showed great courage but understand this man's boss will come looking for us. We'll have to leave El Paso tonight," said his father.

"No, Papa. We don't leave." His son had been thinking. "Stay here. I must go see someone."

The gang boss' hacienda bordered the slums. A ten-minute walk brought the boy to the building. Several men sat at a large wooden table outside, smoking and talking. Wine bottles and food plates scattered among the ashtrays. The boss watched the lad approach. He stopped and took a deep breath and spoke directly to the leader.

"Señor, I am Manuel Estrada. I am the one who killed your man at the plaza today. He wanted the flowers I bought for my mama's birthday. My mama's birthday is more sacred than my life. Do what you will with me."

He managed to hold back the tears that would flood his eyes if he let them. A couple of the men stood up.

The boss motioned for them to sit down. He stared at the boy for a moment.

"How old are you, boy?"

"Thirteen years, Señor. Fourteen in October."

"Where is your father?"

"I have no family, Señor. I left home when I was eight."

The gang boss burst out laughing. The others didn't understand what he found so funny but joined in the laughter.

"Well, my brave Señor Manuel. So, you're an orphan? But you buy flowers for your mama?" More laughter. The man's eyes started to water, and he brushed it away with his sleeve.

"You're the first orphan I know who has a mama and a family right here in the district. I've heard of your father. He's a good man. And he has a son with the heart of a lion. The fool you met today is no loss to me if he can't take care of a thirteen-year-old boy with a bunch of flowers."

He roared again, this time the others joined in, getting the joke at last.

"Señor Estrada, go home to your family. I'll cause no harm done to them. In fact, I'll come with you."

Some of his men stood up, but the boss motioned them to stay. This visit, he would do alone. He collected two bottles of wine and joined the boy.

His father was startled when the gang boss appeared at his door, but relaxed when the man asked him to bring glasses.

Much later, the gang boss walked back to his hacienda, unsteady on his feet having emptied the wine bottles with the senior Estrada. The next day, the boy went to work with his new employer, the most powerful gang boss in El Paso. Thirty-seven years later, Estrada carried the same tag.

# CHAPTER 39

The hospital receptionist signed for the floral delivery, a beautiful bouquet of red roses. The envelope pinned to the present was addressed to Mrs M. Calder.

"Lovely flowers here for Mrs Calder," said the receptionist to the trainee nurse. "Can you take them along to her room?" The young girl picked up the bouquet.

"I wish somebody would buy me flowers like these, they're gorgeous," she said with a grin. Her older colleague smiled back.

"Ah, love's young dream. You'll get plenty of these soon enough, I'm sure."

The girl walked toward the private ward area. Halfway along the corridor, the envelope fell from the flowers. She stooped and picked it up. The envelope was thicker than the normal greeting card.

*Oh my, I hope it didn't get dirty.*

She brushed the envelope with her finger and thumb to remove any imagined dirt. It was the last act of her life. The pressure from her hand movement on the envelope triggered the spring mechanism wedged inside the card. The detonation killed the nurse instantly and set fire alarms clanging throughout the hospital.

Alan Rennie and Jack made their way to May-Ling's room. The corridor where the device had exploded thirty minutes earlier was cordoned off. The men had to circle to the side entrance of the private wing. Rennie's guards stood aside as their boss and Jack entered the room. Doctor Spencer stood at the bedside conversing with his patient.

"Gentlemen."

"Doctor, this is bloody disastrous," said Jack in a rush. "One of your people killed with a bomb meant for my wife. I can't tell you how sorry I am. We can't leave her here now. It's too dangerous for everybody."

He stepped toward May-Ling.

"Sweetheart, how are you? This is terrible. Are you okay? Doc, when can we move her?"

The physician held his hands up in a signal for Jack to slow down.

"Not so fast, Mister Calder. Your wife isn't going anywhere. She needs careful medical attention which this hospital is committed to provide. By the way, Mrs Calder also tried to make a case for leaving. That's not going to happen, unless, of course, you both want to go against my orders. Security will be stepped up. I'm sure Mister Rennie will agree that's feasible? If we run and hide every time some nutcase decides to threaten a medical centre, we'd all have to close down tomorrow."

"I agree," said the police chief. "After this attack, we wouldn't expect another here and I've already ordered extra security from the perimeter inward. Part of your hospital is now a crime scene, and we'll guard it accordingly for at least another week or so while the forensic guys do their job. I'm very sorry about the nurse's death."

"Alan, we know this is Duval's doing," said Jack. "Forensics can look all they want, but we need to find this bastard. And quickly."

"Can I talk to Jack and Alan alone for a few minutes?" said May-Ling in a quiet voice.

"Of course," said the doctor, walking to the door. "I'll be outside."

The two men came nearer to the bed.

"Yes, baby. How are you now?"

"I'm no worse than I was before I heard the explosion. Doctor Spencer is right. I asked him to let me leave, but he insists otherwise. I think we'd cause more problems by moving. Alan gave you his opinion. The police will do what they have to do."

The Assistant Commissioner nodded his agreement again.

"You're also right, Jack. We know who's behind it. I've been thinking this through."

She tried to move a little where she lay to get her bandaged head more comfortable. Jack propped the pillow and tucked in another behind.

"You just stop thinking stuff and get well."

"No. Listen to me. These people murdered Jules and Cy. They tried to get me at the same time in the station. This thing today probably wasn't meant to kill me, but to make a mess of this place. A warning for you to back off. It's tragic the young girl died. Duval may be the front man making the hits, but Fadi and Estrada are calling the shots. Fadi because we busted his business last year. We also arrested his men and cleared out his haul from the jewellery bombings."

May-Ling paused to get her breath.

"Enough," said Jack.

"Hear me out. Cy was killed because of the strike in Turkey, not for what he's done in El Paso. Which confirms these guys are partnering up. This won't go away unless you stop the top honchos. Then you settle with Rikko Duval. Now, Alan here, and Marcel, will do what they need to do on the formal level, but if I'm not mistaken, if you, Malky and the others need to bite more into this new partnership's business, I'm sure they'll make things available to us."

"I won't condone any wild vigilante action, but May-Ling's right," said Alan. "You understand how Marcel and I work with issues like this, Jack. We're hamstrung in many respects in what we can and can't do to counter these people. But helping the wheels of justice roll a bit better is always possible. Just make sure we're kept in the loop."

He stood up and moved to the door.

"See you later."

"That's not all I wanted to say," said May-Ling when Alan had gone. "Doctor Spencer told me he talked to you about how you're handling this."

Jack grunted and shook his head to deflect her comment.

"Sure, you've seen worse trauma than this. Don't let it get too personal, Jack. Remember what Jules taught us. A cool head thinks clearer. Despite what I said just now in front of Alan, Duval's going to keep after you and the other guys. Don't wait for his move. Get on the front foot. He's clever, but my husband's smarter."

Jack embraced his wife gently.

*God, how much I love this woman. Why does it always take life-threatening shit to make me aware of that? Why is she always right?*

"I'll start working on some things tonight, sweetheart. I love you." He kissed her and left the room.

Her body hurt all over, not only on the left side, her shoulder ached, and her leg muscles screamed at her, but her mind was more settled now. Her man was in a better place than an hour earlier.

*Thank you for the alert, Doctor Spencer.*

# CHAPTER 40

"Word from Marcel's boys in Turkey says Fadi's disappeared," said Paul Manning. "I spoke with Alan this morning. The watchers at the villa in Kilyos reported a convoy of cars leaving the compound yesterday. They think the place is empty."

The boardroom smelled of strong coffee. Malky and Jack buddied in their usual seats next to each other. Donnie sat nearest the door.

"Any idea where he's headed?" said Jack.

"Not yet. They've got a spotter at the airport, but nothing showing. It was too risky to tail them right away, but they don't think he's gone into Istanbul itself."

"Why not?"

"They headed off west on the major ring road. It could take them anywhere. The direct route into the city is the dual carriageway south," said Paul.

"Needle in a haystack time," said Donnie. "We can't nail a guy if we can't pin where he is."

Malky leaned forward. "Excuse this ould Irish eejit, but maybe the most obvious place he'd go to keep his head down is home."

"Kilyos is his home," said Jack. "What are you talking about?"

"No it's not, ye daft Jock. Kilyos is where he *lives*. Nobody's ever seen him, right? I reckon he's originally from somewhere else in the region. Someplace ye can drive to. We just have to figure out where."

"He might be right," said Donnie.

Jack gave his partner a play punch on the shoulder. "Once every ten years you come up with a good idea, you know that?"

"How do we fathom likely bolt holes? This whole region's porous," said Paul, stepping up to the wall map and tapping the area with his finger. "He could be across half a dozen borders in a day's drive."

"There might be a quick way to find out," said Jack. "I've an idea if Alan Rennie'll go along with it."

"Tell us," said Donnie.

Jack outlined his thoughts and waited for a response.

"Worth a try," said Donnie. "Let me call Alan."

Ten minutes later the former Scottish cop told Jack, "Green light. He's aboard. Only you and Malky to go."

Jack picked up his jacket and pulled at Malky's arm.

"Let's go."


"You understand this is not official. Everything will be totally deniable?" Assistant Commissioner Rennie spread his fingers toward the ISP men. "Desperate situations need practical solutions, Jack. These hands of mine are tied. But I'm only a policeman."

The unspoken message was clear.

"This is not happening, Alan. It's got nothing to do with you or the Met. Right, Malky?"

The Irishman nodded. "Right, ye are."

"The room at the end of the corridor of the basement below is the only one occupied," said Alan. "No-one else will be around for the next two hours, or until you come back here to my office. Here's the key."

"It won't take that long, Alan. I can promise you," said Jack.

Malky led the way, carrying a small leather bag. As Rennie had arranged, the basement corridor was deserted. The key turned easily in the solid, wooden door and the security men entered. The prisoners each sat on a plastic chair. A plain interview table secured to the floor split the room in half. Jack slammed the door shut. Malky placed the bag on the table and moved toward the smaller man. Jack stepped up to the other.

"Stand up," he ordered.

Both men did as instructed. Each received a sudden hard kick to the groin. The attack caught them by surprise and each slumped forward. Malky steered the smaller one back into a sitting position on his chair. Jack's target was not so lucky. The Scotsman grabbed the stricken man by his shoulders and head-butted him fully across the bridge of the nose, smashing the bone in one movement. A strangled moan escaped as the blood streamed down his shirt and trousers.

"That's just to get us warmed up, gentlemen," he said.

They were too shocked to resist as Malky took a roll of grey duct tape and wire cuffs from the leather bag. The cuffs secured their wrists behind them. The tape strapped their legs to each side of their chairs. Unlike his partner, the smaller man had his mouth taped, with barely enough breathing space at his nose.

Jack's man was conscious but breathing heavily from the effect of the head-butt. His nose bled a little less but spurted again as his aggressor grabbed a handful of hair and yanked his head back. The ceiling light dazzled him.

"Pay attention," said Jack. "I want you to understand I'm pissed. Really pissed. You know why? Because you and your fucking boss did some fucking bad shit on my patch. But it's worse than that."

The man stared, trying to comprehend who these people were.

"Your asshole pals tried to kill my wife. Now, we know your boss is Mister Ahmed fucking Fadi. You know and we know, he's not from Turkey, don't we? Don't we?" Another tug at the hair.

"What you're gonna tell me, so we can stay friends, is where does the shithead go when he's not in Istanbul? You've got five seconds."

The man shook his head.

"Dunno what you talking," he mumbled.

Jack double-slapped the man so hard his head swung violently from side to side.

"Lost your memory, asshole? Let me tell you, my wife might lose her eyesight because of you bastards. This'll help you remember."

He held the man's head back with another vicious pull on the hair and jabbed his thumb hard and deep into the left eye. The prisoner screamed.

"For fuck's sake, man. Ease up. You'll kill him," said Malky, mouthing a rehearsed good guy, bad guy exchange.

"Who cares. He's a piece of shit, anyway."

The smaller prisoner's terror showed in his eyes. Jack delivered a swift punch below his victim's nose, calculated enough to knock him unconscious. The blow caused the man and the chair to topple over. Jack stepped back from the inert body, still tied to the seat. He moved toward the second man.

"Well, I suppose our buddy here's gonna have to talk to me," he said.

Malky ripped the tape from the terrified man's mouth.

"Don't hit me. I can tell you what you want," he said. "Don't hit me."

"This better be good, Mister," said Malky. "My pal here gets off on this stuff."


"Forty minutes. What did I tell you? Wouldn't take two hours," said Jack to the Assistant Commissioner. "Here's the key. One of your lads downstairs fell and hurt himself on the floor. Very careless. He also smacked his eye. The other lad's carrying a bruise or two as well. Must have bumped each other down there."

Alan Rennie took the key and picked up the phone to Bob Granger.

"Okay, Bob. We got what we need. Get a doctor into the cell and fix our friends. Thanks."

He put the phone down.

"Did you get everything?"

"Yes," said Jack. "Nothing you can use in a courtroom. Defence lawyers don't like you leaning on their clients, right?"

"If these guys think Jack might come back to say hello, my guess is they won't be singin' to anybody," said Malky.

"The base is in Tuzla in North-East Bosnia," said Jack. "Our man's real name is Viktor Bodan. He's Serbian. You might want to have Marcel check the name. We've got a fix on where he stays there. The place backs on to the River Jala, so he needs only to protect the front and sides, I suppose. It's about five kilometres west of the town centre, beside a post office and across from a Catholic church, Saint Joseph's.

"What're you going to do now?" said Alan. "Although I think I've a fair idea."

"You keep these boys downstairs isolated for a few days just in case they whisper to lawyers or anybody else about our session today. We'll be in Tuzla within forty-eight hours. We'll talk directly to Marcel about local assistance from his people," said Jack, stretching out his hand.

"Thanks, Alan."

On the drive back to ISP, Malky kept his opinion to himself, but it was the first time he'd ever seen his mate wreak gratuitous violence on anybody. Together they had spent a career in situations where killing was routine, part of getting the job done. Something had changed in Jack Calder. The added attack on the second man after he'd spilled the information was controlled rage.

*This shit's got to him.*

Within twenty-four hours, Interpol confirmed information to Alan Rennie and ISP. Activity at the house on the riverbank in Tuzla. Several vehicles in the front courtyard of the house and many male occupants. No sign of any females. From time to time, one or two cars left, to return a couple of hours later. Other transport arrived carrying various men, many of whom departed after varying periods inside. At least two of the visitors ranked as active in the Serbian underworld. Informed opinion pointed to Ahmed Fadi's alter ego, Viktor Bodan renewing contact with old alliances.

Marcel Benoit aired his surprise at how soon Jack wanted to act.

"No time like the present, Marcel," he said on the secured line to Lyons. "We're all set to go, this time tomorrow night. Myself and the team are going in from the river. If your lads can cover the front in case anybody spills out, that should be enough."

"Jack, my boys estimate at least a dozen men inside."

"The last thing Fadi's expecting in Tuzla is a visit from us. One of Jules' things was always to do the unexpected. Four's plenty to get the job done. Any more will be a crowd, and mistakes can happen in a small area. Trust me on this."

"I trust you, Jack. No doubts on that score. I'll have my men in the church across the road from the house. What do you need from me?"

"A couple of two-man dinghies with strong outboard motors. We'll board them about a half a mile down river. You know the kind of weapons we like. AK 47s are good and some grenades. Can you do these?"

"No problem. Transport'll be waiting for your flight at Tuzla airport. The same on the return journey. Good hunting."

Jack addressed the others in the boardroom.

"Marcel's confirmed Fadi's in place. We're set."

* * *

The best way to ensure an honest partner is to keep him alongside. Manuel Estrada rang the number Fadi had given him.

"I've decided the best way for us is to carry on as planned, amigo," he said.

"I'm pleased to hear that," said Fadi.

"Why don't you come visit. The agency people are putting a lot of heat on the street here. My supplier in Colombia's getting edgy. Maybe you and I take a trip to Bogota and make some friendly head-to-head with him, no?"

"I'm not comfortable in territory I don't control, my friend."

"Don't worry. We've done business with these people for a long time. Security's no issue. Bring some of your own men with you. I'll do the same."

"When do you propose to go?" said Fadi.

"I can arrange a meeting by the end of this week. The sooner the better, no? You can fly tomorrow and be there the next day."

The European took a few seconds to answer. If he declined, the partnership wasn't going to fly. The building pressures from the other side with Interpol and ISP tipped the balance.

"We'll catch a flight tonight. Where to meet in Bogota?"

"I'll book a few rooms for you at the Paradiso Hotel."

"Done, partner."

"Adios."

Fadi called his lieutenant to his room.

"Yes, boss?"

"We need flights to Bogota for you, me and two others."

# CHAPTER 41

Minimal delay at Tuzla airport meant more time to check the weapons in the rear of the van as they drove to the river. Marcel's flawless arrangements included black overalls and headgear. The driver took the vehicle along the road passing Fadi's location. Jack wanted to get his bearings before proceeding to the riverside. The church faced the two-storey house, thirty metres across from the grey-painted front. A few cars were parked outside but with no personnel in view. Lights on the ground floor and a couple of rooms on the upstairs level shone halfway across the road. The building stretched back no more than ten metres toward the river. Original use of the place would have served a large family, expansive by local standards but of modest dimensions.

*Smallish area to clear out. Glad we stuck to a compact strike force. No doors at the side. Good. It means there must be an entrance at the back. No other houses close by.*

The dinghies carried normal outboard engines. The distance to the rear of the house needed nothing more powerful. Paul climbed in beside Jack. Donnie and Malky boarded the second. They slung the AK 47s across their backs and carried grenades in the overalls' pockets. Calf-strapped daggers completed the weaponry, with no intent on taking prisoners. A hunt and kill mission.

A long, slow arc brought them opposite the house. More lights showed through the curtains upstairs at the back, to all appearances a full house. Paul steered his dinghy ten metres left, cut the outboard and let it drift into the bank. Donnie did the same ten metres to the right. First out, Jack and Malky covered the others as they pulled the dinghies upside. From a crouching position they had a clear view of the outside perimeter. Malky pointed toward a guard sitting alone on a bench near the back door. A modern version M16 lay alongside a clutter of empty beer bottles and a full ashtray on the small table at the side. The remains of supper plates sat next to the bottles.

*The guard hadn't produced all that litter by himself. Where was the backup?*

The sentry raised another beer bottle to his mouth and tipped his head back. The man heard nothing as Jack covered the few metres to his quarry. A sharp karate blow to his exposed throat interrupted his swallow and seconds later a snapped neck sealed his fate. The other three approached. The sound of two men talking filtered toward the doorway. Donnie and Paul met them in one movement. Their unexpected presence gave the two former cops the edge as dagger slashes to the throat stifled any noise. They dragged the bodies outside to join their dead companion and entered the corridor as a foursome, AK 47s at the ready. The hallway extended three metres toward an opening into a large sitting area, passing a stairway leading to the upper floor level. The four-man chevron crept closer. A quiet buzz of conversation mingled with the sound of a television program. Jack estimated eight men in the large room as the team stepped in. He and Paul fired off from the centre to the left, Malky and Donnie taking from the centre to the right. In such a tight area aiming wasn't needed. The combined fire power swept the area in seconds. Bodies slumped where they sat or fell to the floor where they'd been standing. Paul and Malky waited at the door of the room in case they'd missed anybody. Jack and Donnie covered the two paces back to the stairwell. The clatter of boots thudded toward the top of the wooden banister. Jack lobbed a stun grenade up as he and his partner stepped to the side wall to avoid the blast. Screams of panic mixed with the sound of further movement. Three men lay across the upper landing and top stairs, disoriented by the stunning. A short burst from the AK 47 ended their confusion. Further noise indicated a hasty retreat of three or four others. Donnie passed Jack on the stairwell and threw another grenade up and along the upper hallway. Moments later the blast rocked the place again. The attacking pair mounted the stair in double steps, firing non-stop on the way. Only two men lay on the carpet, already felled by the deluge of bullets. Near the end of the corridor, a door slammed tight. All the other room doors were open. The prey was trapped in one chamber. Jack aimed at the door handle and let loose several bursts. The locking mechanism and the wood surrounding it disintegrated. The door swung inward a couple feet. Rapid fire from inside the room splintered more of the door as bullets ripped outward, causing it to slam shut and open again as it bounced against the lintel rim. The range of shooting from inside was confined to the borders of the door. Jack eased along the wall and threw in another grenade. Silence followed the explosion. Donnie crouched and peered into the room. One man was dead already, another dying beside him. Two shots to the head hastened his departure.

Jack and Donnie covered each other in rote as they cleared each of the remaining three upstairs bedrooms, even checking wardrobes. Satisfied to find no further occupants, they joined their partners downstairs.

"Anybody still breathing?" Jack asked Malky.

"One guy over here, but he's not gonna last more than a few minutes. He's the only one," said Malky, pointing to a badly injured man, sprawled across a blood-stained sofa. Jack knelt beside him.

"Which of you is Ahmed Fadi?" he said.

The man stared back at him and tried to shake his head.

"Tell me, which one is he?" Jack repeated.

The man moved his head again and tried to speak.

"Viktor? Viktor? Viktor left yesterday. Fuck you," he managed to whisper.

A grotesque half-smile twisted at the man's lips. His head lolled to the side as blood trickled from his mouth and the stare of death fixed across his eyes.

Malky walked across to where the man lay and tugged at his sleeve.

"You missed something, Jack. Look at his hand." The right hand stuck out from the sleeve, the bare skin showing all the way to the wrist.

"Well, I'll be damned," said Jack. On the skin was a defined birthmark they'd seen before, resembling a large, spilled coffee stain. The killer of Martha Compton and ISP's accountant in Berlin would kill no more.

The grainy copy photograph taken of the man with Estrada in Boston didn't match any of the bodies in the house.

"Fuck," said Jack. "The bastard's right. None of these guys is Fadi. Where the hell's he gone?"

"Wherever it is, he won't be back here now," said Paul Manning. "It wasn't a lost effort, Jack. This'll rattle him. He won't know where to expect us next."

"Maybe, but we need to find him soon to keep him on the back foot. We can't hit somebody we can't see. Donnie, get Alan and Marcel up to speed with this. Tell them we're still hunting."

The Interpol agents ferried the squad back to Tuzla airport and waited until after the plane soared into the sky before making a call to the local newspaper.

The red-herring message was simple. The agent told the journalist he represented the families of those killed so many years ago by the criminal guerrillas. If the police did their jobs properly, they wouldn't have to do it for them.

"Mister Bodan thinks he can waltz in and out of this place along with his scum whenever he likes. We don't like ethnic cleansing. There will be more retribution."

The false plant would keep the authorities chasing shadows for months.

# CHAPTER 42

The direct request from Manuel Estrada to Carlos Silva to make available a floor of suites at the Paradiso Hotel in Bogata was easily fulfilled. Silva owned the hotel. His companies' portfolios also had several other property developments in the city. The Silva family had grown into the largest single supplier of cocaine in the world. The third -generation son, Carlos held sway over a far-reaching international corporate empire. His father had ensured a solid business education for his first-born by sending him to Harvard for four years. The investment paid enormous dividends. The sharp acumen gained from the best financial tutoring available combined well with the family reputation for deal-making. The effect of modern techniques for identifying money laundering were countered with equally ingenious mechanisms to evade detection. Layers of chains of command protected Silva from even the most minor prosecution, but he still called the shots. Major business decisions and relationship-building needed his approval. The proposed visit from Estrada suited Silva. The Mexican's trade over many years had proved highly profitable. The recent disruption in El Paso from the DEA heat had caused concern. This would be a good time to hear from the principal's mouth how he intended to address the situation.

The camera clicked repeatedly, recording the departure of Manuel Estrada from the same airport where Cy Foster was killed. The watchers inside noted the Bogota flight details for onward notification to their counterparts in Colombia.

Similar to his status in El Paso, the Mexican wasn't subject to any arrest warrant in Bogota. The limousine transporting him to the Paradiso attracted surveillance, as with his regular previous trips to Colombia. The authorities knew where to find him but held no legal reason to do anything other than track his movements.

The camera followed the Estrada group's exit from the vehicle. They walked a few paces into the shade of the large vestibule fronting the hotel and stopped. The drug boss looked at his watch and appeared to be waiting for someone, checking a couple of times on cars arriving at the hotel driveway. After some minutes, a Paradiso courtesy limousine drew up in front. The long-range Nikon shots captured a repeat of the meeting at the Boston Four Seasons.

Ahmed Fadi shook hands with his host and accompanied him into the hotel.

* * *

Five hours later, a refreshed Ahmed Fadi had slept and showered. He was ready to discuss business. The entire top floor had been vacated to afford maximum privacy for both visiting groups. The sitting area in the lounge held only the two of them. Their henchmen sat forty metres away at the other end of the room.

"It's good to see you, Manuel," said Fadi, embracing his counterpart. "How is your family after the dreadful loss of your dear daughter?"

"We are all grieving, amigo, but none more than my wife. She's been under heavy sedation since the murder. But business must go on."

"Agreed."

They sat down on closely adjoining armchairs out of earshot of the guards, trading niceties over coffee.

"You mentioned a proposal involving your supplier here in Bogota," said Fadi.

"Yes. Carlos Silva. We're all his guests. This is his hotel. I told you on the phone, I've done business with his family for many years. I have a long-standing contract to buy a fixed percentage of his production. With the nonsense recently in El Paso, for reasons you well understand, the arrangement has come to a temporary halt. Carlos is aware of the DEA's assaults on us. He gets a lot of that in Colombia too, but he has so many ways to get around it locally," said Estrada reaching for the coffee pot. "More coffee?"

Fadi held his cup out for the refill. "Is he putting pressure on you?"

"No. Not yet. But his patience won't be unlimited. He's mentioned an offer of a large shipment of cocaine. I believe he's testing my resolve, amigo."

"How big a shipment?" said Fadi.

"Wholesale price, two hundred million dollars. You can figure yourself how much that's worth on the street."

Fadi pursed his lips. "That's a lot of money. What payment terms does he propose?"

"Cash. Carlos is a friend, but he's also a tough businessman. He never deals on credit, not even to me."

The Mexican emptied his cup and sat back in his chair. His new partner sipped at his own cup and placed it on the table.

"When does he need an answer?"

"We're his guests for dinner an hour from now. By the time we finish tonight, he'll expect our response. I need to know your position before we meet him."

"I take it you want me in as an equal partner with you? A hundred million dollars? Cash?"

"The stuff shipped to Antalya was peanuts, amigo. You agreed yourself it was meant only as an operational trial run, not a full-blown commercial deal. We know who the bastards are who hijacked us. That won't happen again. It's time to do some real business. We do this deal with Carlos and ship to dozens of distribution lines on your side and mine. Even if these British bastards are stupid enough to try us again, we'll be ready, and they can't cover all the places we can."

"I admire your thinking," said Fadi. "A hundred million's more than I'd normally put in one shot."

Estrada held his gaze. Decision time.

"I'm in. Tell me where to send the money." Fadi smiled and extended his hand. He didn't share with the Mexican the news he'd received before this meeting about the slaughter of his people in Tuzla. His position was steadily weakening. He needed guaranteed supplies. Estrada needed alternative distribution streams. The sooner the better.

A private dinner in the owner's quarters in the hotel was an eye-opener for Ahmed Fadi. Compared to Manuel Estrada, Carlos Silva oozed class. The immaculate Italian tailoring of his suit, the well-polished shoes and conservative shirt and tie would have been at home in a Wall Street chairman's office. Fadi guessed his age at touching forty, some fifteen years junior to both of his dinner guests. There was no doubt, however, he ranked as the senior partner at the table.

"Manuel informs me he has a new business associate, Mister Fadi. Welcome," said Silva.

"Call me Ahmed, please," said Fadi. "I'm honoured to meet you."

"Ahmed it is then. Let's eat. I believe we do business better on a full stomach. Come, sit."

Fadi watched as his companions ordered juices to drink. No alcohol. He followed their lead. At dinner back at the Four Seasons in Boston, Estrada had shared wine with him. Silva obviously didn't mix pleasure with business. The meal passed pleasantly until waiters served the coffee and retired from the dining salon.

"Ahmed, I like to talk straight to my business partners," said Silva. "Manuel tells me you're good for your hundred million dollars. I trust his word, but I also take nothing for granted."

Fadi nodded. "You're a careful man, Carlos. I respect that. I guess you want to see the colour of my money in your accounts before we move forward?"

Silva smiled and nodded in turn. He removed a folded sheet of paper from his jacket pocket and handed it to Fadi.

"I already have Manuel's payment. On here you'll find a list of twelve banks with different account names and separate amounts assigned to each of them. The total is a hundred million dollars. I expect the funds to be in these accounts within twenty-four hours. Otherwise, I don't have a new partner."

Fadi glanced at the list, folded the paper over and put it in his own pocket. He stood up from the table.

"Gentlemen, thank you for a most enjoyable dinner. If you'll please excuse me, I'd like to go make a phone call. I'll ask you to check these accounts within twelve hours, not twenty-four, Carlos."

Fadi shook hands with both of them and left the room. He wasn't able to see the grins on each of their faces after he'd gone.


The call to his accountants confirmed the money transfers had been executed as instructed within twelve hours.

*These smart asses wanna play bullshit macho money games? Two of us can play that way. What do they think I am? Some fucking cheapskate?*

He walked from his quarters to Estrada's at the other end of the floor. The Mexican sat behind an ornate desk in the living area of the suite. Three of the Mexican's men sat on chairs against the wall. Estrada used a stiletto to slice open a couriered package as Fadi arrived.

"Good afternoon, Ahmed. Take a seat," he said, pointing with the blade to the large chair in front of him. Estrada put his feet up on the desk and leaned back.

"My people confirm the money's been sent," said Fadi.

"I know. Carlos called to tell me. He likes things done properly," said Estrada. "So do I."

Fadi heard a click and turned his head. One of the guards held a pistol to his neck. A second and third pulled his arms backward and fastened handcuffs on his wrists.

"What the fuck?"

The gunman holstered his weapon and walked behind Fadi. He slipped a garrotte round his throat and pulled it taut. The wire bit into his skin below the Adam's apple but not enough to restrict his breathing. Manuel Estrada swung his legs to bring his feet to the floor and walked around his desk. His eyes burned with rage.

"I'll tell you what the fuck, you murdering bastard," he spat. "You think Manuel Estrada's some dumb asshole? First you lose my fucking shipment and blame me for the fuckwits you employ."

The garrotte tightened. Fadi tried to speak but could only manage a strangled, guttural noise. His eyes watered and his head began to spin.

"Then you feed me the story the British guys killed my daughter," said Estrada. "The black guy arranged all of this, right? Listen, you fucking son of a whore. The DEA and the British don't go after kids. Unlike you, you pile of shit. I checked you out, Ahmed, or whatever your fucking name is. You've pulled crap like this before. Carlos Silva confirmed it for me before you came. I told you he's a careful man. It's his business to know about scum like you."

The garrotte drew blood as Fadi began to lose consciousness. Despite his blurring vision, he saw Estrada come closer.

"You killed my beautiful little girl, you bastard." Estrada drove the stiletto into Fadi's belly and ripped upward with enraged violence. He withdrew the weapon and stabbed again and again, each blow driven as hard as the Mexican could manage. He waved away the man with the garrotte and plunged the blade through Fadi's throat with so much rage, the point of the stiletto exited from the back of the man's neck. The object of his hatred died well before the final stabbings.

"You know what to do with this piece of dog shit," he said to the guards, walking back to his seat behind the desk.

The instinctive gnawing doubt he'd felt when Ahmed Fadi called with his condolences had grown into a realisation of who was responsible for his daughter's murder. He reached for the desk telephone and rang Carlos Silva.

"Buenos dias, amigo. The scum's taken care of. We'll find ways to move all the shipment into the States. Maybe we use some of your routes as well as mine. Mister Fadi's contribution is much appreciated, no? I'm going back to El Paso later tonight. I'll be in touch."

The farmer kept his distance. A van had appeared at the far side of his field. Three men bundled four large bags at the side of the verge and drove away. He called the local police number without giving a name and went to work in another field at the other side of his homestead. It wasn't good to get involved in other people's business in Colombia.

# CHAPTER 43

Donnie broke the news to the group. "You're not gonna believe this lot. Alan rang me. He and Marcel have been on the wires for the last couple of days. The cops in Bogota picked up four dumped bodies, a common event with the drug gangs. No IDs on any of them. They ran fingerprint checks locally and came up empty, so they ran them through Interpol and found two of them have criminal records in Serbia going back twenty years. The DEA lads had a look at the photos of the stiffs on the off chance it might trigger some ideas. And who do you think one of them was?"

Malky chimed in. "Go on, Santa Claus on holiday."

Jack and Paul started laughing.

"Just as wild," said Donnie. "They reckon it's our friend, Ahmed Fadi, lately known to us as Viktor Bodan."

"What?" said Jack, looking at his partner in astonishment.

"More than that. Three of the corpses had a couple of bullets in the head, quick execution style. The one they think's Fadi was a bloody mess. Wire-strangled body with multiple stab wounds and a stiletto through his throat. Somebody wanted to mangle him big time."

Nobody was laughing any more.

"Yer man does a runner from us in Bosnia and ends up toast in Colombia?" said Malky. "How does that fit?"

"Fadi met Estrada in Bogota. The DEA boys got them on camera," said Donnie. "All friendly on the surface when the pictures were taken.

Sure as hell there won't be any evidence to tie the killings into Estrada, but can you bet against him doing it?"

Jack was pensive. He rubbed his chin and shook his head.

"Where's the sense in Estrada knocking off his new partner?" said Paul.

"Jules was bang on the money," said Jack. "Fucking them over in Turkey means they kicked off mistrusting each other. God only knows what happened afterward. Unless." He paused. "Unless Estrada's pinned Fadi for the hit on his daughter."

Donnie whistled. "Plausible. That would explain the stabbing violence. The last time we had one of those in London, a husband went knife-crazy on his wife's killer. Attacks on family can do strange things to people."

"Tell me about it," said Jack.

"I'm sorry, Jack. I didn't mean…"

The Scotsman waved the comment aside, but a resurgence of anger against his wife's attackers welled up.

"It's okay. You're right," said Jack. "Whatever way, one out of three's done. Our Mister Estrada's not going far from El Paso. I wonder how much he doles out in bribes to keep him secure? The bigger puzzle is where to find Rikko Duval."

* * *

"What are the ISP people doing now?" Marcel Benoit asked the Assistant Commissioner.

"I met Jack Calder earlier visiting May-Ling," said Alan Rennie. "He's pissed they didn't nail Fadi at the house. The news from Bogota didn't seem to please nor displease him. He hinted at having a crack at Estrada next. How would the DEA guys react to that?"

"I understand they had a couple of joint forays already about a month ago," said Marcel. "I think they'd be more than welcome. You and I might not be able to operate in London or Lyons the same way as they can in El Paso. We've discussed this before, Alan. Sometimes you have to fight fire with fire."

Local newspapers in Bogota carried nothing on the deaths of the four Serbs. Journalists' desire for personal survival in a city rife with corruption, fed with money from wholesale drug trafficking activity, motivated the self-censorship. Carlos Silva headed the biggest network, but his was only one of several large organisations whose principal revenue generator was supplying cocaine to the rest of the world.

The DEA had other ideas about reporting the killings. Television channels in the United States and Europe picked up stories fed to the international press, courtesy of the agency, with gruesome pictures of Fadi's mutilated body and three dead henchmen. No names of suspected perpetrators appeared in the articles. The agency wanted a simple, primary message carried. A major international drug trafficker had been killed. Any death at that level was a positive score in the war against drugs.

* * *

Another continent away, in a rain-soaked Manchester, Rikko Duval switched off the television. His paymaster was dead. He'd underestimated Manuel Estrada and sent Fadi on a fatal wild-goose chase. The attack on the Bosnian house was fading news. Local revenge killings, according to the Bosnian press. Duval thought otherwise. He recognised the work of professional assassins. Calder was following Townsend's lead.

*Too bad,* he mused. *Shit happens. I'm not recognisable on any of Fadi's records. The money's invisible now. The payments traced to Gibraltar carried the Robert Cavendish name, but that fucking photograph on the television must have come through Jules. Which means ISP's still a problem. These fuckers know I'm the only guy able to rig the deals in New Bond Street and King's Cross. A pity the hospital hit missed the target. So, what to do next?*

Duval was coming up empty with answers. And his knee hurt. He walked to the bathroom for his painkillers. The mirror showed his beard almost fully grown. The purchase of brown-tinted glasses had helped change the eye line. For the moment the rented flat in Manchester served his need for anonymity. The north-western city, the second most populous in England, swallowed him up along with thousands of others.

*If you want to remain hidden, stay in a crowd.*

The former soldier had no links of any kind to the metropolis. Nothing to lead anyone to him. He could take time thinking about his next move.

# CHAPTER 44

Hank Turner, second-in-command to Cy Foster, stepped up one link in the chain after his boss was murdered. A seasoned agent, his six-year tenure in El Paso-Juarez stretched back two years before Cy's appointment. He had enjoyed working with the ISP men during the week of their previous visit. When Jack Calder rang, he was pleased to take the call.

"Jack, how're you doing? I see Mister Fadi bought his, this week."

"Good afternoon, Hank, or I guess, still morning with you guys. Yes, we just missed giving him our regards in Bosnia."

"So I heard. Good job. To what do I owe the pleasure of your call?"

"We'd like to help in nailing Estrada. I realise you can't legally arrest him in El Paso. Besides, if I don't miss my guess, he's probably got a major investment in the local police force?"

"Yup. Makes things kinda tricky. We hit the down-line activity almost daily. Lower-level people are expendable to guys like Estrada. And for every success we get, in come replacements. Men and drugs."

"For us to come in under the radar would be tricky," said Jack. "Not impossible, but tricky. We'd prefer a situation with higher odds of success. A better deal would be if somehow we can flush him out of Mexico."

"I'll keep my ears open. We've a few paid informers helping with snippets, but nobody high enough to keep us up to speed with the big man's movements in detail."

"Maybe we can help with some grease money. How about a hundred thousand dollars?" said Jack.

"Hey. That kind of money might produce something. Let me work on it."

"We just want to be alerted if and when he leaves the country and where he's going. A hundred grand to tell us that much should make something happen."

"I'll get back to you. Have a good day, my friend. Goodbye."


"They let me out of bed for the first time this morning," said May-Ling. "A couple of lengths of the room."

"How did it feel?" asked Jack.

"Shaky. For the first few steps, I thought I was going to fall."

Jack's anxiety showed. His wife caught the look on his face.

"Oh, Jack. It's okay. The physiotherapist checked me out. She reckons I'll be up and about in days. She says I could be out of here in two or three weeks. Stop worrying."

"Stop worrying? Baby, you get hit by a bomb blast, part of your eyesight's at risk, you're lying here, and I'm so fucking helpless. Of course, I'm bloody worried."

He stood up and paced the floor, angry for letting his emotions show in front of her.

"Come here, you silly man." She reached out with her right arm, the left still difficult to move with the shoulder injury, and he leaned over the bed to embrace her. "I love you so much."

His eyes welled up and as much to hide any tears from her, he brought her close and held her tight, more than ever determined he would nail that bastard Duval.

*Donnie Mullen was right, when someone hurts your family, no other feelings of rage come close.*


Patience is part of the deal, Duval reminded himself.

He prided himself on the ability to wait. To wait for the optimum moment to execute his own strategy in his own time and at his own pace.

For twenty years he'd operated solo. No partners to screw up. No family to take into account. Of course, his forward planning had always included an ultimate bolt hole. The right amount of money could buy access to many safe, welcoming domiciles. Wealthy foreigners prepared to give up some of their capital to their adopted havens would always find a home. The trick lay in identifying a place to stay anonymous. Armed protection could be bought. He had enough money to live well for the rest of his life.

The presence of Jack Calder and ISP cast a long shadow on all these plans. Somewhere, sometime, they'd find him. Even if they didn't, he wouldn't sleep easy in case they did come, wherever in the world he might be. A chance coincidence, a routine check by local cops, nosy neighbours, and the whole game would change.

*Who'd have thought the fucking bank manager was a risk?*

Survival depended on eliminating the risks as much as possible. His former comrades-in-arms posed the biggest danger now. He had to take care of that threat sooner or later. Patience. He didn't have an answer now but would find one if he worked at it long enough.

*They'll be expecting something. So, take your time and do it right, Rikko.*

# CHAPTER 45

"We've got something for you, Jack, but not from the source you'd suggested," said Hank Turner. "We pitched some feelers in El Paso. I thought a hundred grand would've found some takers, but nothing from there yet. Maybe they're all too rich already. More likely they're scared shitless about blowing the whistle on Estrada." The long-distance line cut and Jack waited for the reconnection.

"What've you got?" said Jack.

"My counterpart's informers in Vancouver brought him something late last night."

"The Mounties?"

"Yes sirree, the good old Royal Canadian Mounted Police," said Hank. "The whole of the Canadian west coast drug trade's run by the Chinese. More than half of the Drug Squad's Asian. They've had a deep plant in one of the major gangs for years. Only feeds big stuff to them. From all accounts, highly reliable. The noise says Estrada's visiting next week. Tuesday evening arrival. We think he's been distributing into California and all the way up the continental west coast for a while, but never had any concrete proof, as usual."

"What's to say you'll get any incriminating evidence if he's just visiting?" said Jack.

"Nothing. We've no record of Estrada ever travelling as far up the coast. Makes me think something big's about to move when he feels the need to be involved personally. I discussed you guys with my pal in the

Drug Squad up there. He'd have no problem with any intervention, but obviously can't back you openly."

"Understood. We can work around that. I'll need some location details, players, likely storage hides, the standard stuff."

"You'll have it within the hour, including contacts with the Mounties in case of need. Good luck, Jack."

"Thanks, Hank. I'll be in touch."


"We're going to Canada, Malky," said Jack. "Our man's moving north to ride shotgun on a load of shit. Five days from now. Hank says he wouldn't be bothered for small stuff. Odds are on a major load going into Vancouver. It's pretty damn cold this time of year, so get your woolly drawers ready."

"We all coming?" asked Donnie.

"The fewer the better on this one. The primary aim's to take out Estrada. One man and a back-up's plenty. You and Paul can keep the rest of this place sane."


The contact details from Turner gave Jack the direct connection with the local Drug Squad chief. A half-hour telephone link brought the promise of weapons supply, and an unmarked car with instructions where to leave the vehicle after any action the ISP men might engage. All discussion was off the record. To be able to claim non-involvement in any black operation, the chief suggested not to meet when Jack and Malky landed. If things went wrong, there was a number to call.

A day later, detailed location maps to the proposed drugs storage site arrived. Jack decided they'd travel to arrive in Vancouver a day earlier, on Monday afternoon.


The temperature flirted around zero. Jack and Malky exited Vancouver International Airport with a chill wind whipping at their legs. The packed exit hall confirmed the airport's reputation as the second busiest in

Canada. The nearest North American mainland airport to Asia, it could have been mistaken for Hong Kong with the scrum of Chinese faces in the forecourts. The ISP men carried only hand luggage to the short-term car park. The black Chevrolet Express cargo van with the coded number plate sat fifty metres from the far corner. Malky reached under the rear wheel bay and removed the envelope containing the keys. Inside the van, they checked the bags with the weaponry. Automatic pistols, AK 47s, and grenades of choice. Everything as requested.

The journey downtown in late afternoon traffic crawled. They were in no hurry. The Mounties had arranged prepayment for two nights in a nondescript three-star hotel. Jack and Malky intended to stay for one. The flight over the Atlantic and the American continent had offered enough sleeping time.

The afternoon half-light had disappeared into a starless evening when they re-emerged an hour after checking in. Malky drove out toward the north of the city. Their destination lay no more than ten kilometres from the hotel. A cluster of warehouses bordered the main road. Some carried signage, others none. Three back from the highway stood a timber-clad hangar-sized building with several elongated glazed openings ten metres from the ground. The front entrance held roll-open, roll-shut sliding doors with drive-in width of several metres, enough for two vehicles to pass together. The Polish name above the opening declared Joseph Jodlowski Freight Forwarders. The Warsaw connection had long since given way to Chinese ownership.

Malky parked the Chevrolet thirty metres across the street and cut the lights. Most of the other warehouses slept in darkness. The commercial park didn't waste money on unnecessary street lighting. Illumination beamed from the top of the Jodlowski warehouse but the entrance was shut. A collection of trucks and pick-up lorries surrounded the place, with a handful of passenger vehicles. The building stretched back fifty metres. Close to the rear, dimly lit from the top lights, a pile of packing cases bordered an external generator. Several oil drums with fuel for the generator lined the side of the building.

Jack trained the night-vision glasses from the vantage point across the road. A small truck drove up and the driver tooted his horn three times. The doors rolled open to let the vehicle in. The binoculars gave a clear view inside the warehouse. The centre aisle gave uncluttered access all the way to the back, room enough for half a dozen vehicles. Assorted stacking racks and pallets sat on each side. At the rear on the right a wooden stair with a handrail attached to the back wall led up to a boxed-in office. A couple of motorbikes parked inside near the gate. Apart from these and the lorry, no other vehicles occupied the interior. No sign of personnel meant anyone inside the building was in the office.

"Drive around to the back road," said Jack. "The map says there's a wall all the way across, but let's check it anyway."

The map proved accurate. They'd seen enough to get their bearings and Malky headed back to the hotel. Their information had Manuel Estrada arriving the next evening.


The Mexican's business needed the push from Carlos Silva's supply. The squeeze in El Paso continued to curtail cash flow. The hundred million demanded from the Colombian had cleaned out his liquid reserves. This foray had to work. In the early days, building the distribution networks was part and parcel of Estrada's hands-on approach to the business. This deal needed no hiccup, and he'd decided to handle it directly. Local connections provided private quarters for him and his guards. Estrada carried no weapons, but his entourage of three men did. Minders met the plane as early evening encroached and ferried the group to the safe house where a brief freshening-up preceded the convoy's journey to Jodlowski's warehouse.

Hours before the group set off, Jack Calder and Malky McGuire were already in place opposite the building, farther back across the roadway than the previous day. They left the hotel and spent fifteen minutes in the back of the cargo van changing into black clothing and double-checking the guns. Malky kept to the speed limit, retracing the reconnaissance trip. The commercial estate sat in from the main highway, with sparse traffic inside, as only vehicles with deliveries or collections to make came into the area. Similar to the previous day, the Jodlowski warehouse doors remained closed, although vehicles outside and lights from the high window slats showed it was occupied.

Daylight segued into early evening. A dark-red Lexus arrived and gave the three horn-toots signal. The entrance rolled open, and the car entered and parked well inside the warehouse. Nobody closed the door, indicating to the watching pair the imminent arrival of someone else. Two Asian men got out of the front of the car. One held open the rear door, and the boss stepped out. Another guard joined them. All except the top man carried Uzi sub-machine guns. The boss led the way up the stairway to the office. One sentry, also armed, stayed downstairs, inside the open doorway.

Jack and Malky didn't have long to wait for the next arrival. A white van and a Ford Capri drove up and joined the Lexus inside. The sentry rolled the door shut behind them.

"What d'ye bet that's the payload?" said Malky.

"Yup. Hardly bring armed guards to deliver a pizza, huh? Now all we need is Mister E. to come to the party."

# CHAPTER 46

Eight months before Rikko Duval's bomb killed Jules Townsend, ISP disrupted Ahmed Fadi's drug business by intercepting a huge shipment of Afghani heroin. Fadi's prized sixty-million dollar luxury yacht had also been forfeited in the raid twelve miles off the coast near Portsmouth in the south of England. Part of the hit squad included Paul Manning. At the time of the strike, he was in the process of rebuilding his reputation within the Metropolitan Police. For several years he ran the SWAT operations in and around London, his many successes unfortunately offset by a couple of bad experiences on his record.

His determination to put things right included a situation where he saved Jules' life in a shoot-out in Albania with some of Fadi's partners. He retired from the force with his reputation recovered and approached Jules to join the ISP team. Jules and the rest of the squad welcomed him into the company, and he became a valuable asset.

Paul had never married and embraced the environment with his former Met colleague, Donnie Mullen, and the ex-SAS men with enthusiasm. In the same way, a few years earlier Donnie had enjoyed the freer licence afforded to ISP than the restrictive procedures the police had to work under. The new lease of life was a far cry from the cloud Manning had been under for the couple of years prior to getting involved with the security firm.

Other than the current focus on the drug gangs and Rikko Duval, the firm had an extensive international business to run. Donnie had asked

Paul to join an early morning meeting in the office at seven-thirty with a prospective new client from Switzerland. He listened to the television news as he washed down the usual light breakfast of toast and some fruit with strong coffee. Nothing of special interest to the firm. No word yet of activity in Vancouver, which was eight hours behind London's time zone. He fixed his tie and checked in the hallway mirror. Old police habits are hard to shake. Uniform or not, professional appearance is always important. The drive into the office this time of day varied from thirty to forty-five minutes depending on traffic. He closed the door behind him at six-thirty and walked the few metres to his car in the driveway. A slight frost misted the windscreen, not enough to prevent safe driving. He got into the car, pulled the seatbelt over his shoulder, and turned the ignition key. In the still of the suburban morning, the explosion echoed over a mile away.

The rented car pulled away from the corner. Rikko Duval didn't need to wait to be a part of any crowd massing at the dead man's garden gate. He drove slowly, avoiding pieces of twisted metal thrown across the street. Several vehicle and house alarms wailed in unison as he turned the corner and headed south toward the port ferry terminal to Europe.

*That'll slow the bastards up.*

# CHAPTER 47

In Vancouver, the temperature slid below freezing. In the Chevrolet, Jack and Malky's gloves and protective jackets kept the cold at bay. A running engine might draw attention. They wore black balaclavas with only the eyes showing but sat back from the windscreen to avoid chance detection. Jack reckoned they'd only get one real shot at this tonight, and they'd make it count.

Headlights from two cars swivelled into the area and pointed in toward the warehouse. No horns sounded and the vehicles parked a few metres to the side of the entrance. Malky switched on the cargo van's engine and eased onto the verge opposite the sliding doorway. Three men got out of the cars and waited for the last man. The bulky figure of Estrada climbed from the rear of the second car and was immediately flanked by the others. The mist from the condensing air from their breath rose in small clouds from each of them.

"Wait," said Jack. "Not yet."

The door rolled open a couple of metres and the Chinese boss appeared with two of his men. He walked toward Estrada and held out his hand to greet his visitor. The two drug bosses exchanged some words and started toward the doorway.

"Ready," said Jack. "There's at least another six inside, minimum a dozen in total."

"Ten-four," said Malky. He caressed the accelerator with his foot, waiting for the signal.

The outside group reached the opening, and the door was pulled further ajar. A wooden trestle table at the side of the central aisle was stacked with silvered, foil-wrapped packages. The shipment was ready for checking. The bosses reached the table, followed by the henchmen. Estrada's men's M16s matched the Uzis of the Chinese gang.

"Go!"

Malky slammed hard on the accelerator. The sentry on the door was slow to close the sliding mechanism behind the group. At the last second, he looked up at the van speeding toward him. He backed away from the doorway and screamed a warning. Malky brought the Chevrolet skidding to a halt in the doorway, smashing sideways into the left door shutter, preventing it from moving. The guard raised his weapon at the intruders. The burst from Jack's AK 47 ripped his chest and throat and he fell across the door entrance.

Malky gunned the van into reverse a couple of metres. Jack lobbed a stun grenade forward. When the alarm shout sounded, Estrada and his Chinese counterpart sprinted toward the rear of the warehouse. The guards had no time to aim before the explosion hit them. Jack and Malky dismounted firing rapid salvoes. Jack threw a second grenade where he'd seen Estrada go and fired through the smoke where the guards had fallen. None of them would survive the onslaught. From the rear, two figures emerged, dazed by the shock of the stun grenade.

Malky's round lifted the Chinese boss off the ground. The Mexican put his hands in the air but was met with several bullets in the skull from Jack. Estrada's body continued to twitch where it lay as Jack continued firing at him.

*Fucking overkill,* thought Malky. *Guess he's gotta get it out of his system.*

The pair moved back toward the Chevrolet. Upstairs, the door to the office swung open. Two men exited, crouched and fired.

"Upstairs, Malky," Jack shouted, raking the assailants with gunfire. He hit the target and both men collapsed.

"I'm hit, Jack. Fuckin' leg, dammit."

Jack jumped across to where his partner sat against the front wheel of the van, blood oozing through the bottom of his trouser leg. He used his knife to cut away the lower part of the cloth.

"Incomin'," Malky yelled. He raised the AK 47 and fired, killing the last pair of guards coming out of the office. The blood flowed heavily from Malky's lower limb. The bone was smashed.

"No way you're flying the Golden Skies tonight, lad," said Jack. "How many hit you?"

"I only felt one. I think I'd know if it was more. Bastards."

Jack used the trouser cloth as a makeshift tourniquet. The wound wasn't life-threatening.

"Okay. Into the van," said Jack.

Malky looped his arms around Jack's neck as the big man lifted him into the passenger seat. The blood flow had stopped. Jack reversed the Chevrolet and spun it around to face the roadway. He got out of the vehicle and walked to the side of the warehouse and tossed a grenade into the stack of oil drums. He retraced his steps to the front door as the oil drums exploded and lobbed another under the table with the cocaine stacked in expensive piles.

The van headed out toward the fallback rendezvous earmarked in case of any slip-up.

"Unless they can filter cocaine dust out of fresh air, they won't make any fucking money out of that load," he said as the second detonation obliterated the dead Mexican's shipment. The rear mirror captured the flames racing up the timber walls of Jodlowski's Freight Forwarders warehouse. Jack glanced across at Malky. His partner had slipped into unconsciousness. He flipped the mobile phone open, dialled the back-up number and got an immediate response.

"I've a man down. Leg bleeding from a bullet wound. He needs a hospital in a hurry."

"Ten-four on a man down. We'll be with you in six minutes."

The promised six minutes matched Jack's arrival time at the secluded rendezvous. The Mounties' Drug Squad men helped Malky out of the van and into the ambulance which drew up within a further one minute.

"Thanks guys," said Jack. "Look after him for me. He owes me a drink."

The Canadians smiled at the universal gallows humour peculiar to law enforcement officers and military.

"He'll get the best attention the RCMP can offer. Where you heading now?"

"Got a plane to catch. Oh, and by the way, you guys just busted a ton of shit at Jodlowski's warehouse. And your morgue's gonna be a bit crowded tonight. See you later."

He shook hands with the lieutenant-in-charge and drove off toward the airport.

*Two down, one to go.*

# CHAPTER 48

Donnie chauffeured Jack from the airport direct to May-Ling. The injury to Malky had already taken the shine off the success in Vancouver. The news of Paul Manning's murder hit Jack hard.

"Bastard. I fucked up. I should've gone after Duval first," he said.

"Cut it out, Jack," said Donnie. "Nobody's got a clue where he is. Not you, not me, not Marcel, not Alan Rennie, none of us. The old needle in the haystack bit. Now his paymaster's gone. His money's not in Gibraltar. The man could be anywhere on the planet."

"So, what do we do? Sit and wait until he blows us all away one by fucking one?"

"Calm down. You're not gonna help any by losing your cool every ten minutes. I want to nail this guy as much as you do. Chasing shadows isn't the way go."

"Then what do you have in mind?"

"Right now, priority's on protecting ourselves," said Donnie. "And our people, Jack. They're at risk too. I ordered the office in London closed until further notice. We've done that before and can operate out of Amsterdam without too much disruption. I reckon because we senior guys are the main targets in this nutter's head, London's the most likely target centre."

"Do we have *any* idea where he is?"

"Yesterday, while you were in the air, Marcel's people traced a CCTV image of a man with a limp disembarking from the ferry in Ostend. The close-ups show a guy with a beard and glasses. Not an infallible identification, but Marcel's ninety-nine percent certain it's him and he's in Europe. They're scouring Holland, Belgium and France as we speak."

"The problem with that is so long as he doesn't go walking around in public much, the man's so fucking ordinary-looking," said Jack.

"By the way, Alan's stepped up the security again at the hospital. Look."

Donnie parked the car and they walked toward the entrance. The police presence included officers in the parking area. The receptionist nodded recognition and waved them through to the private ward area. They turned the corner into the long corridor leading to May-Ling's room and Jack stopped dead in his tracks. His wife, assisted by a nurse on either side, was making her way along the hallway.

"Hello, darling," she said, with a lop-sided smile. "I told you I'd be out of here soon."

Jack hugged her gently.

"You go and sit inside. I'll be there in a few minutes. Let me finish my exercise," she said.

The nurses brought her back ten minutes later. Instead of getting back into bed, she sat in the armchair. The cards and get-well messages surrounded the room. Only flowers brought in by Alan Rennie himself were allowed. Donnie waited outside with the guards.

"How're you feeling?" asked Jack.

"That's the third time they've let me walk the length of the hall and back. The first time was terrible, but today felt good. I need to keep the muscles moving."

The bruising on the left side of the face was fading, but the bandages still covered her damaged eye. Medical dressings adorned the left leg and shoulder, with added strapping around her knee.

"What's the doc saying about the eye?"

"Still too early to predict how it'll be, but the blood clot at the back of the retina's cleared. They do the checks a couple of times a day. When they take the bandage off, things are still blurred. The specialist says it won't be clear until the internal bruising subsides. We have to wait and find out whenever they say I'm ready."

"The baby? What about the baby?"

"Everything's normal, Doctor Spencer says."

Jack reached across and hugged her again.

"And of course, we've lost Paul," he said.

May-Ling looked puzzled.

"Paul? What's happened to Paul?"

Her face showed nobody had told her yet. Donnie had forgotten to warn him.

"Oh, shit. I'm sorry, darling. Paul was killed yesterday morning."

"How? Duval? Oh, no," she whispered.

Jack held her. Her body shook. Not telling her had been the right thing to do, and he'd messed that up.

"I'm sorry, baby. I didn't know they hadn't told you yet. I guess it's better coming from me, anyway. On the plus side, we nailed Estrada, but Malky took a bullet in the leg. The Canadians are looking after him."

"Jack, this won't stop until you find him. You know that don't you?"

"Yes. We're working on it. Donnie's trying to keep me cool. He says the priority now is to protect ourselves. You, me, the rest of our people, and he's right. On all counts. We think he's back in Europe, but we're not sure."

"What are you going to do now?"

"First things first. I'm going home to get some sleep. I'll catch up with Donnie later. We've closed the office for the rest of the staff meantime. They can operate from home for a few days until we work out what to do next. I'll be back tonight, sweetheart."

She walked with him to the door and kissed him goodbye.

Donnie headed the car toward Beckenham to drop his partner home.

"You never told me she didn't know about Paul," said Jack.

"Oh, hell. Sorry, mate. Mea culpa. Major slip up. We kept the news from her, thinking she doesn't need any extra stress worrying about the rest of us. I fucked up."

"Don't worry, she's strong enough."

"Catch you up later this afternoon. I need some sleep. I'll call you when I'm awake," said Jack, retrieving his hand luggage from the back seat.

Donnie waved and pulled away from Jack's gate.

The suburban semi-detached had been a big step-up from his bachelor flat in St. John's Wood. A married man with a family needed something more practical than the pad he'd used more as a parking slot to sleep in than a home. The search for value for money meant moving out to a locale favoured by the professional set. Beckenham ticked all the boxes for he and May-Ling when they returned from Hong Kong with a ten-year-old son. Now, eight years on, it would soon welcome a new baby. He pushed open the gate and dug in his jacket pocket for the front door key. A meowing sound at his ankles distracted him from putting the key in the lock. The Siamese cat from next door, a regular visitor to the Calder household, purred and rubbed against his leg.

"Hello, Mimi," he said and bent to stroke the animal's head. "Nice to get a welcome home." The cat's ears flapped back, and the purring increased.

"You'll take any amount of that, won't you?"

Jack froze. From the lower angle, he sighted a thread-thin cord looping from the bottom of the door. He picked Mimi up and backed away to the end of the pathway. The cat continued to purr. The mobile phone fast-dial flicked to Donnie's number. It rang several times without answer.

"C'mon, answer the bloody thing, man." Now Mimi nestled at his chin. Donnie's voice came online.

"Sorry, Jack. I was at traffic lights. What's up?"

"Duval's been here."

"What? How?"

"I haven't touched the front door, but there's a thread coil at the bottom corner," said Jack.

"Damn. You know the drill. Touch nothing. I'll call Alan and get the bomb squad moving pronto. I'll be back with you in a few minutes."

Jack put his luggage bag on the ground to sit on. Mimi was in no hurry to leave him.

First to arrive, Donnie checked the doorway and eased back down the pathway as Alan Rennie and DCI Bob Granger appeared.

"Classic trigger cord, Alan," said Donnie.

"Duval must've tracked your movements, Jack. He knew you weren't here," said Alan. "I've sent a team over to your place, too, Donnie. Better safe than sorry."

Several police vehicles pulled up, including the bomb squad specialists. The back-up team went into a well-rehearsed containment drill.

The police asked the occupants of several houses either side of Jack's place and those across the street to leave for their own safety. Blue and white tape stretched across the roadway at both ends. The neighbouring couple who owned Mimi both worked in the daytime. The cat stayed in Jack's arms.

"You've a key for the backdoor too, I presume?" said Bob Granger.

"Yes," said Jack, handing the key to the detective. "For fuck's sake, tell these lads to be careful. We don't need any more losses to that bastard."

"They know what they're doing, Jack. Relax," said Bob, walking away to talk to the bomb squad leader.

The rear entry to the house held no traps, but the two specialists moved cautiously through the hallways, checking the floors for pressure springs. The hall rug behind the front door lay crumpled to one side. At the bottom of the door frame a metal canister pointed forward. The coil ran from the base across the upright wooden support and taped on to the door itself. Any movement inward would trigger the mechanism. The same type of device had killed Jules Townsend. The leader checked for any decoy phantom wire and found none. The wire cutter snipped the coil clean to deactivate the bomb.

"Roger. Clear one," he said to his partner. "Let's check the other rooms."

Jack waited in the police van with Alan Rennie and Donnie. Someone rustled up some coffee and doughnuts. Mimi found a new parking place in Donnie Mullen's lap.

"If Mimi hadn't been here, you'd be picking bits of me off the road," said Jack.

The Assistant Commissioner smiled. "Wasn't meant to be your time," he said.

"The lads at Donnie's place've called in all clear. For the next week or so I'm posting officers at both your homes. I'll get them over to Malky's place too."

"That's not necessary," said Jack. "We can look after ourselves."

"You just acknowledged, if Mimi wasn't here, neither would you be," said Alan. "I have a duty to protect the rest of the public here as well, Jack. The officers stay."

The television cameras turned up halfway through proceedings. By the time the specialists satisfied themselves the entire house was safe, it was already late afternoon. The police allowed the other inhabitants to return to their homes, but not before the newshounds had milked the story dry.

"Let's can the meeting for today, Donnie. Catch up early tomorrow. I've gotta sleep."

"Sure. Goodnight."


A brief call to Canada assured Jack his buddy was receiving the best of medical attention. He'd be on a plane back to London in a week. Dusk settled on the street as he drew the bedroom curtains closed. Outside his front gate an officer stood watch. He thought he imagined a few curtains opposite twitching as he looked out. He walked to the back bedroom and gazed out on a second policeman on duty at the rear gate.

*What the hell's wrong with this picture?* he asked himself.

A long, steaming-hot shower took away some of the fatigue of the past few days. He collapsed into bed and fell asleep in seconds.

For many years before meeting May-Ling, Jack had recurring nightmares, a throwback to visions of his late father's suicide in a filthy, flour-bagging cellar in the slums of Glasgow. Jack had been seven years old, but forty years later he couldn't shake the taste of dust and the riveting death stare from his Da's eyes. Interchanged with these came horrific re-casts of barbaric scenes encountered during under-cover assignments in the jungles of Africa and Indo-China. May-Ling had helped him exorcise these by sharing how she'd coped with her own horrendous nightmares after the untimely killing of her first husband in a street battle with triads in Hong Kong. They had been in the force together. His death had been a tragic example of being in the wrong place at the wrong time.

Jack hadn't suffered bad dreams for over fifteen years. Tonight, they came back in droves. Half asleep, he sat upright trying to shake off the top sheet, fighting to get at the sneering face of Rikko Duval. The bomber had the bloodied head of Jules Townsend in one hand and a grenade in the other with the pin removed. Jack grabbed at Duval and fell to the floor, the jolt wakening him completely. He lay for a few moments, covered in sweat, until reality returned. Sleep was impossible for the rest of the night. The gremlins danced in his brain. He had to act on Duval. Waiting for his adversary to make the next move was driving him crazy. He'd call Marcel in Lyons this morning.

# CHAPTER 49

Jack felt like death warmed over. Another hot shower had done little to ease the tension from his shoulders. As the dawn broke, he realised he hadn't eaten properly for almost twenty-four hours. A ravenous appetite was blunted with a huge, cooked breakfast. It also gave him something to do until time to go visit his wife. The police officer at the front gate nodded a good morning greeting as Jack got into his car. The journey took longer than usual with a couple of road accidents en route holding up the traffic. The icy conditions always produced bottlenecks and he was glad to get to the hospital with only a forty-minute delay.

Schedules for patients never paralleled those of the outside world. May-Ling had been awake since five o'clock. Her first therapy of the day started at seven, completed with more walking in the corridor. This time she needed only one nurse to keep her steady. Doctor Spencer stood by the bedside when Jack arrived.

"Morning, Doc. Morning, sweetheart," he said, kissing his wife on the forehead.

"Good morning, Mister Calder. She's making excellent progress. Frankly, I'm surprised at how soon her strength's returning."

He removed a thermometer from May-Ling's mouth.

"Hello, darling. How did you sleep? You're like something the cat brought in."

"If it hadn't been for the cat I wouldn't be here, baby."

The quizzical looks from both his wife and the doctor held a ton of questions.

Jack explained the events of the previous afternoon and why he hadn't come back in the evening.

"My God, Jack," said May-Ling when he'd finished. He hadn't mentioned the nightmare.

"I'm sorry to hear this," said the doctor. "I hope the authorities catch this madman soon. I'll be back later, Mrs Calder."

Jack didn't miss the concerned glance the doctor gave him before leaving the room.

He hugged his wife. This time she held on longer than usual before sitting down again in the armchair.

"I spoke with Marcel this morning," said Jack. "No reported sightings yet. They've circulated the CCTV pictures of Duval from the ferry terminal at Ostend with his changed appearance, as well as the original stuff Mac gave Jules. Sooner or later the bastard'll slip up."

"I've been thinking, Jack. Some of the training courses we did back in Hong Kong covered the psychology of loners. Rikko Duval's a one-off. No family. No relationships. No associates. He doesn't need money. Jules said he was like a chessmaster."

"Honey, this isn't a game."

"Hear me out. Chessmasters operate on logic. They win by out-thinking their opponent's moves."

"So?"

"It also involves moving to where you're least expected to be. We've been trying to figure out likely hiding places for one guy. Usually, large crowds can serve the purpose, but only for so long. Then he'd have to move again. Where's the least likely place you'd expect to find him?"

Jack stared at May-Ling for a few seconds as he absorbed her logic. Then he spoke. "Jeez, sweetheart. You could be right."

He jumped up from his seat and embraced his wife.

"It might be a while before I'm back. I love you, baby."

"I love you too, Jack. More than you'll ever know. Be careful."

# CHAPTER 50

Rikko Duval gave the beret an extra tug over his brow. The long coat concealed the limp effectively. The vantage point across the street afforded a clear view. No lights and no movement for the past hour. He walked across the road and swung the gate ajar. Moments later the front door opened and he entered. In the darkness of the hallway, he reached for the light switch and flipped it on.

"Welcome home, Rikko."

The man sitting on the chair facing the door raised his arm and fired. A searing pain burned across his chest and Duval collapsed to the floor. The taser gun wires snaked back to where Jack Calder sat. The shock of fifty thousand volts to the human body incapacitates the muscles for up to seven or eight minutes. Duval was helpless to prevent the Scotsman's actions.

Jack dragged him onto the seat and secured his legs to the front. The plastic slide-cuffs bound his wrists behind his back. Duct tape rolled several times around his torso, leaving no room for leverage from the chair. He wrapped the tape twice around his neck and jerked backward, looping the end to the top spar of the chair. The final piece taped his mouth shut.

As the feeling came back into his limbs, Duval could do nothing. Jack unrolled a cloth package and extracted a half-brick of familiar reddish-orange material and several tiny tubes of artist's paint. Semtex in malleable form looks like builder's putty. At first, he couldn't fathom what his captor was doing with the paint. Red, green, blue, yellow, white. Then he understood. Bright colours. No camouflage. He mumbled in vain. Jack Calder's mission was unstoppable.

One by one, parcels formed in Jack's hands. Rikko Duval wasn't the only one with SAS Semtex training. Into each, a small detonator completed the explosive biscuits, ranged in colours like a birthday cake. The duct tape affixed each one to the terrified mercenary's body, all on the left side. The significance was lost on him until Jack strapped the last parcel tightly over his left eye. Now he understood.

No amount of struggling made any difference. Jack Calder arranged more Semtex parcels around the room, all positioned to channel blasts toward the chair. Duval watched as his intruder tidied the used paint tubes into the cloth bag, placed the bundle under the seat and strolled to the end of the hallway. He didn't look back.

Jack closed the door and made his way to the street, mounted the motorbike parked fifty metres away and kicked the engine into life. He took the radio transmitter from his pocket, switched to live mode, pointed at the villa, and pressed the button.

Fed with planted snippets from Interpol, the Casablanca press carried news of the discovery of a rogue terrorist cell of indeterminate source. Something had gone wrong in a bomb factory in a villa in the city suburbs. The obliterated remains of at least one body were being tested for DNA, but the wreckage inside the house had been so devastating, authorities held little hope of identification. No other casualties were reported.

# CHAPTER 51

A month after the blast in Morocco, Chuck Morrow, in his capacity as chairman of the Society of Re-Insurance Groups, delivered on the contract with ISP. A Manager's Check for ten million dollars from the society complemented the generous payouts already made to ease the burdens of families caught up in the New Bond Street bombings.

The ISP partners agreed unanimously on the disposition of the windfall. Half of the contract money was placed on various term deposits and working capital accounts for the firm.

Other disbursements included handsome amounts to the relatives of the ISP personnel killed in Hong Kong and Frankfurt.

The grief-stricken parents of the dead nurse received a payment in memory of their daughter.

In the name of one of their own, former head of Serious Crimes Division, Paul Manning, further money found its way to Alan Rennie at the London Metropolitan Police with instructions to seed a fund for families of officers killed in the line of duty.

A large sum in the shape of an endowment to the Intensive Care Unit found grateful recipients at the hospital where May-Ling was treated.

Jack drove his wife home two weeks after returning from Casablanca. Rehabilitation was far from complete, but she had made enough progress to satisfy Doctor Spencer to authorise her release from hospital. A walking stick helped the daily routine of long walks until the leg muscles strengthened enough for her to do away with the cane. Her husband's arm became a more welcome substitute morning and evening as the strides became brisker. Twice-weekly visits to the physiotherapy unit accelerated her recovery.

The fear of completely losing her eyesight receded. The retina would need a series of reconstructive operations to recover almost seventy-five percent vision. The bump in her belly had become noticeable by the time Jack brought her home and was expanding every week.

Six weeks passed and Jack ferried May-Ling to the office where the rest of the partners waited in the boardroom. Malky's injury was on the mend. He sat at the end of the table with his leg sticking out, encased in a plaster cast.

"Hello," said Donnie, kissing May-Ling on both cheeks. She leaned forward for Malky to follow suit.

"It's wonderful to have you back, looking so well," Donnie continued. A smile danced across his face. "We need you present today for an important board item."

May-Ling frowned, bemused.

"We've been discussing how to re-organise ourselves with Jules and Paul gone. Your injuries, especially to your eye, makes it impractical to think you'll be on field duties in the future. You're also carrying another little Calder. The rest of us would appreciate you considering becoming chief executive officer of the firm."

"I'm flattered, Donnie, but surely one of you men…"

"No," Donnie interrupted her. "None of us has your perceptive qualities. Jules always said you were the brightest spanner in the box. We're all boots-on-the-road guys. We need a steady head directing us. You know how we work. An outsider isn't an option. Oh, and by the way, Jack had no vote on this."

Everybody laughed, including May-Ling.

"But the baby?"

"You wouldn't be the first chief executive to take maternity leave. We can live with that if you can. Will you accept?"

"I guess you give me no choice. You're so persuasive."

"I think I'll call this meeting closed," said Donnie. "A celebratory lunch is in order. ISP pays."

# CHAPTER 52

Alan Rennie collected Marcel Benoit in person from the airport for the drive to Winchester. The Assistant Commissioner wore civvies, no match for the neat European cut of the Frenchman's suit. The shop talk was inevitable. Since the disruption of Fadi's and Estrada's empires, new drug-lord pretenders disputed the rights to the business.

"They're like bloody cockroaches," said Alan. "No matter how many we eradicate, another swarm's always ready to pick up where they left off."

"Keep the faith, my friend," said Marcel. "Think how it would be if we didn't at least keep putting down the current crop. In Turkey, we've had dozens of mob killings over the fight for the Afghani trade."

"How about El Paso?"

"Hank Turner told me this week one of Estrada's competitors is making deals with the others. Some sort of agreement to cartel. That's more problematic, I'm afraid."

"I wish we could utilise guys like Jack Calder more," said Alan.

"So do I, but you know as well as I do, our government lords and masters won't buy in. The politically correct brigade's too loud. Vigilante nonsense they say. So long as people like us run what we do, Alan, we've always the means to give the quiet nod to the likes of ISP."

"Amen to that. Here's the cathedral."

Malky opened the rear door to permit Jules' widow to get into the car. Instead, she beckoned her children inside. She preferred to sit in the front passenger seat alongside the Irishman. Throughout his career, Jules had kept his family life a universe apart from his military service and business activity, deciding it was the only way to stay honest to both worlds. Malky didn't even know her first name.

"G'mornin', Mrs Townsend. Mornin'," he said to the children behind him.

"Good morning, Mister McGuire," she said. "It's very kind of you to pick us up."

She had dispensed with her widow's black soon after Jules' burial. The circles her family moved in didn't much dwell on morbidity.

"What a lovely morning for a christening," she said.

"Aye, it's all o' that," said Malky, heading toward the cathedral.

Donnie Mullen's Jaguar appeared in the parking area before anyone else. Old police habits die hard. He wanted to arrive early and take a stroll around, making sure everything was in its right place. The other vehicles began to arrive and lined up alongside where Donnie had left his, a short walk to the entrance.

Mac journeyed with an SAS driver the hundred and fifteen miles south from his SAS base at Stirling Lines. Jack considered him family, as did most of his former colleagues. The dark-blue, double-breasted suit, immaculately pressed, held the empty left sleeve tucked into the jacket pocket, pinned tight with half an inch room on either side.

Twenty minutes before the hour, Jack Calder steered the family Range Rover into the reserved spot closest to the cathedral doors. Tommy Calder, their son, emerged from the front passenger side to open the rear door for his mother. At six feet, he was almost as tall as his father. He took his mother's hand and helped her exit. She slipped her arm easily into Tommy's and he escorted her toward the church. The lifting duty belonged to his father. Jack took the carry-cot from the back seat. The baby lay asleep until Jack moved the cot. Moments later it started to cry.

*Jeez. What is it with me and babies?* he joked to himself.

The walking motion soothed the baby by the time Jack had reached his wife and the other guests. May-Ling lifted the child from the cot. As with Tommy, the blue eyes and blonde hair of its father had been overruled by the beautiful brown eyes and jet black hair of the mother.

Unlike the previous visit to a packed cathedral for Jules' funeral, the Dean officiated for a congregation of no more than thirty people. Godfathers, Malky McGuire, Donnie Mullen, Alan Rennie, Marcel Benoit and Mac complemented the only godmother, Mrs Townsend.

The order of service proceeded and came to the baptismal passage. May-Ling, five weeks after the birth and showing hardly any change from her pre-pregnancy figure, handed the offspring to Mrs Townsend to take to the font.

The baby wriggled its arms, engrossed with the gold and red coloured sleeve of the Dean's cloak as he wet its brow and intoned, "I baptise you in the name of the Father, and of the Son, and of the Holy Spirit…Jules Malcolm Calder."

Jack and May-Ling, with Jules Malcolm Calder, placed the flowers against the headstone and stood for a moment at the grave of their mentor. May-Ling shared Jack's silent tears as baby Jules smiled at both of them.